'Beautifully translated by Marilyn Booth in the poignant, lyrical style of the original Arabic, *Bitter Orange Tree* is a

...rds pro...
revision, too.' **The New Yo...**

'Imaginative ... a bittersweet, non-linear e... 2020 - status and a young woman's agency.' ***A Time*** ...dy. **the Month**

'Alharthi makes lyrical shifts between past and present, memory and folklore, oneiric surrealism and grimy realism.' ***Guardian***

'[A] stirring tale of a woman who battles every social and religious constraint. The juxtaposition with the narrator's reflections on modern life and the speed of change is brilliantly judged in Marilyn Booth's agile translation from Arabic.' ***The Observer***

'An uncommon work of literature with an exceptional translation to match.' ***The Hindu Times***

'A gorgeous and insightful story of longing ... The bittersweet narrative, intuitively translated by Booth, is chock-full of indelible images ... This solidifies Alharthi's well-earned literary reputation.' ***Publishers Weekly***

'An extended examination of the dynamics of nostalgia ... it blurs the lines between longing and belonging in cadenced, lyrical, and poignant prose.' **The Telegraph India**

'From the first Omani woman to have a novel translated into English, this remarkable novel centers the evolution of one woman's agency, power and relationships.' **Ms**

'Alharthi probes family relationships and picks at the frayed edges where the heart and society want different things ... [She] deftly describes the frustration of being between two cultures.' **Hadara Magazine**

'In a global literary landscape that has long centered on male authors working in English, Alharthi and Booth's work with contemporary Arabophone literature feels daring and exciting.' **Electric Literature**

'In probing history, challenging social status, questioning familial bonds and debts, Alharthi's multilayered pages beautifully, achingly unveil the haunting aloneness of women's experiences.' **Booklist**

ALSO BY JOKHA ALHARTHI

Celestial Bodies

Bitter Orange Tree

A Novel

Jokha Alharthi

TRANSLATED FROM THE ARABIC BY
MARILYN BOOTH

SCRIBNER

LONDON NEW YORK SYDNEY TORONTO NEW DELHI

First published in the United States by Catapult, 2022

First published in Great Britain by Scribner, an imprint
of Simon & Schuster UK Ltd, 2022

This paperback edition published 2023

1 3 5 7 9 10 8 6 4 2

Simon & Schuster UK Ltd
1st Floor
222 Gray's Inn Road
London WC1X 8HB

Simon & Schuster Australia, Sydney
Simon & Schuster India, New Delhi

www.simonandschuster.co.uk
www.simonandschuster.com.au
www.simonandschuster.co.in

A CIP catalogue record for this book
is available from the British Library

Paperback ISBN: 978-1-4711-9392-7
EBOOK ISBN: 978-1-4711-9391-0

Book design by Wah-Ming Chang
Printed and Bound in the UK using 100% Renewable
Electricity at CPI Group (UK) Ltd

To the man of wisdom

Bitter Orange Tree

Fingers

I open my eyes suddenly and see her fingers. One by one I see them, fleshy, wrinkled, the nails rough. A single silver ring; and her thumb with its thick, tough black nail, preserving the traces of a bad injury that all but severed it.

I didn't see that strange fingernail as strange. She always asked me to cut it, but the heaviest nail clipper wasn't strong enough. Every time I tried, she would shake her head. "Khalaas. Forget it—try the knife." And a small blade really would appear, all of a sudden, from nowhere, it seemed. I didn't attempt it, though. I cut the rest of her nails, the ordinary, healthy ones, leaving her the business of the hard black thumbnail deformed by injury.

Waking up to snow falling outside the window of my top-floor room in the university residence hall, I climb out of my narrow bed and stand barefoot on the wooden floor in my long nightgown, staring into the snow and the darkness. And suddenly what I am seeing is not the nighttime landscape but the hard, black, crooked nail. Right there, plain before my eyes, leaving me wakeful with remorse. I go back to my narrow bed, and finally the voices of my classmates in the kitchen fade away and the loud music from my neighbor's room grows faint, as I toss and turn in an agony of regret.

I could have done something for the black nail instead of leaving it to grow so long, neglected and askew. It was possible for the word *ignore* not to exist. But it did. It existed and it grew, and it got longer, just as the black nail lengthened, just like any confident, healthy fingernail would grow long enough to leave a scratch or not. Like this nail of mine, still bearing traces of the polish I had put on for my Pakistani friend's birthday party the day before. Yes, the word *ignore* could go on and on—without a nail clipper, without any polish even, and when I felt like I was suffocating, wrapped up in my long nightgown, in my little bed on that snowy night, it was the remorse, the guilt, that choked me. Neglect. Negligence. Looking the other way. Pretending not to notice. Ignoring it.

Was there ever a day when I asked her, "What happened to your finger?" Maybe, but if so, I don't remember what she said, if anything. I remember collecting the rough slivers cut from the healthy fingernails, ready to toss them out. She wanted me to bury them in the dirt, but I ignored her. I pretended not to know that this was what she wanted. She'd tug at her white pouch of medications, concealed beneath her outstretched leg, and hand it to me. There was nothing there one could read, not really, perhaps two or three lines of ink on every little plastic bag. The white pills twice a day, the pink ones three times a day. What were the pills for? I don't know. I never asked. I had twenty problems in my math textbook that I had to come up with solutions for: I wasn't about to start asking questions about the medicines with hurriedly written lines of ink sprawling across them.

I would forget the fingers, forget the medications. Then, on some night, any night, a night without insomnia, or grief, or memories, I would see her in a dream. Sitting, the way she always was sitting during those last ten years, her face sweet and all wrinkles, her smile radiating goodness, her arms reaching out for me. When she stretches her arms toward me in that way she always had, the long, bright-colored tarha draped over her head cascades into dozens of little folds and pleats, and the silver ring on her healthy, straight little finger flashes with light, concealing the afflicted black nail. And then I fall into her embrace.

It would already have been autumn. The large trees ringing the university residence would have gone yellow and the leaves would have fallen. The caretakers would be sweeping the yellowed leaves from the pavements, and the female students would be showing off how well they could endure the colder weather by choosing to wear their shortest skirts. But just a moment before, I had been there: just before I opened my eyes and autumn plunked itself down in my consciousness. I was in her embrace, I was smelling her scent, a blend of civet musk, precious aloeswood oil, and ancient soil. We were switching roles. I was repeating the words that she'd always said over and over: "Don't go." No, we didn't exchange places exactly, because this time she was smiling softly, sympathetically. I hadn't done that back when she was the one saying "Don't go."

I had gone. And then she had gone. And it wasn't possible to change anything. What the hand of fate had written could not be unwritten. That ancient line of poetry: *All your tears, all your pleas, will erase not a line of that which is written.* For I had gone, and I went away without smiling. I just went, in my cocky presumption that I could look the other way. That I didn't know; that I didn't need to know. And then: remorse. Harsh, grating regret, making me more fragile than the brittle autumn leaves crumbling under the janitor's broom beneath my window.

My svelte Pakistani friend's fingers were perfectly symmetrical and polish never touched those nails. Her name, Suroor, means "happiness." And yes, she was the picture of happiness. Suroor: jet-black hair rippling down her back and a dazzling smile. Her slender fingers with the precisely clipped nails raking through that beautiful hair of hers. No scratch ever blemished her nails. It was as if life itself had deposited her in a remote and sheltered spot, protected from storms or high winds. No scratches, no swellings, no scars. I was always teasing her. Looking at her fingers brought ancient poems to mind. "You are made for love, Suroor." She would laugh. In my defense, I quoted the ancient Lubna's beloved Qays, the sad and lovelorn poet.

> *Love's own tokens etch themselves, the*
> *youthful form grows thin*
> *Love will strip from the lover's hands the*
> *very finger-bones*

Suroor didn't like that at all—"the very finger-bones," imagine!—and she herself wasn't made for love. Her sister was.

On her birthday—the day I painted my nails bright red—Suroor's mind seemed to be elsewhere. For her older sister, Kuhl, had married her beloved in a secret temporary marriage. No one else knew, and Suroor had to conceal that severe secret. It was a heavy, heavy weight on picture-of-happiness Suroor. Born in her father's luxurious villa in Karachi, speaking nothing but English all of her carefree life, Suroor didn't know what to do with this knowledge. It overwhelmed her; it perplexed her. She didn't understand how her sister could have gone from a few silly flirtations to the calamitous business of marriage. And for whom? A boy with only secondary school English he had learned in his remote village somewhere deep in the interior of Pakistan. His father wasn't a distinguished banker like hers was, and his peasant mother had never heard of a city called London. But in her final year studying for a medical degree, Kuhl found a shaykh who was willing to bind her and her beloved in a mutaa marriage. And Suroor, on her twenty-second birthday, was bearing the secret, dragging it around with her like a mutilated finger with a misshapen black nail.

Her long black hair falling disheveled over my shoulder, Suroor sobbed. "Just imagine, Zuhour, imagine! My sister . . . my very own sister, marrying that peasant!" Suroor was prettier than her sister; she resembled their mother, who had grown up in London and, had it not been for her marriage, probably would have become a star of the London stage. Suroor didn't wear any makeup. Her tears were pure, clean drops, not darkened by kohl or tainted by face powder. They were large drops, glistening pearls, proper tears: suitable tears. But my tears—they had been thin brownish lines edging down my dirty face.

As my grandmother had rubbed them off my cheeks with her black-nailed thumb, she handed me her walking stick and said, "Go after them! Give them a good beating, will you." I had pretended to go off, but instead I hid in the enclosed prayer alcove behind the main house. It was the summer before she went lame and could do nothing but sit. She was still walking every late afternoon then, between our house and the orchards, cutting across the narrow lanes where we played. And then there came the day when she witnessed a scene that had happened many times before, unbeknownst to her. Me, sprawled on the ground, and Fattoum rolling my face in the dirt while her brother, Ulyan, yanks my hair, and tears run in dirty lines down my face. Suddenly she was there: her massive frame, her distinctive height and full, strong body. The walking stick that always supported her came down on Fattoum and

Ulyan. They scampered away, slipping into their house, but she followed them, and she swung that cane upward and thwacked the wood door, nearly splintering it. When Abu Ulyan opened the door, it was a miracle that he escaped having an eye gouged out by her cane. "If you don't punish those kids of yours," she said, "we will." And she turned away and marched home without as much as a glance at me.

There was still some birthday cake and paper cups half-full of juice on the table. Very few classmates had shown up: Suroor didn't serve alcohol. She was studying classical and medieval Arabic. For a while now, she had been more at ease reading the medieval scholar al-Tabari than she was reading the newspaper. Reading ancient scholars' interpretations of the Qur'an, she'd become convinced that her father was wrong to have served drinks at his boisterous parties, whether at the Karachi villa or in the London flat.

I was thinking that we ought to clean the place up, but Suroor just went on moaning about her sister. "He's a peasant. His mom and dad are illiterate. A farmer." But he wasn't a peasant farmer. He was a student pursuing a university degree in medicine, just like her sister.

"My grandmother would've given anything to be a peasant farmer," I said. And then immediately I regretted my abrupt reaction. Suroor raised her head. "Your grandmother?" Right. The words had come out and they couldn't be put back. I had said it: *my grandmother*. Why don't words come automatically with threads that we can yank to pull them back inside ourselves? But there are no threads attached. Those words had been said. What's done is done.

The Father's Platter

Everything happened in the course of the First World War.

Shipping was at a standstill in the Gulf, and goods were hard to come by. The price of a sack of rice shot up to a hundred qirsh, each qirsh coin the old, heavy silver Maria Theresa thalers that circulated in Oman back then. A bag of dried dates cost thirty. A woman's cotton head-shawl couldn't be had for less than two entire qirsh. Drought struck. Famine. The irrigation canals dried up, the date palms were dying, and whole villages emptied as people left home, heading to parts of the country where hunger was not so widespread or acute, and life was more affordable, or to the east coast of Africa.

She and her brother were born not long after the war, in one of the villages staggering under the burden of inflation and drought. Her mother died of fever when she was only a few years old. These were the years when people were circulating rumors whose source no one knew, about a British company that had been granted oil-drilling rights. Her father was a fine equestrian and a horse trainer, skilled at taming recalcitrant horses. But his new wife tamed him. She convinced him that it was best for the two of them, and for the children they now had, to expel the brother and sister whose mother had died. And so that is what happened. As his son was reaching out for a bit of food from the family's shared platter, the father slapped his arm, and the precious grains of rice flew from the fingers of the fifteen-year-old boy. His sister, two years younger, started shivering and stopped eating. The father began to shout. "Shame! Don't you feel shame eating from your father's platter? Eat from the toil of your own arm! Do you think your father is yours, and yours alone? He's not always going to be here for you."

She told me this story the day she roughed up Fattoum and Ulyan, rescuing me once and for all from having my face rubbed in the dirt and my hair torn out. Yet I didn't believe her. I imagined my own father gripping *my* brother's hand and then putting my hand in his and expelling us from the house. It wasn't possible. Surely such a thing could not happen. But she told the story countless times after that, and every time, one little tear from her single good eye would roll down her face. Not because they'd been kicked out as two lone orphans but in memory of her brother who had not been able to endure the misery and pain of working as a day laborer building mud-brick houses. He died less than two years after their expulsion.

"Your grandmother?" asked Suroor. "She wanted to be a peasant farmer?"

It really is true, one cannot yank the words back, there are no threads attached to them that we can tug, to make them disappear. "She always longed to own some land," I responded. "Just a tiny patch, with date palms growing on it, even if there was only space for five or so. And a few little fruit trees—lemon, papaya, banana, bitter orange. She would even plant those herself. She would water them and take care of them. And eat from them. And rest in their shade."

My friend was silent. She probably didn't have a clue what I was trying to say. We gathered up the cups and plates and wiped the tables clean. The party had ended. Suroor would go to sleep, suppressing the thought of her sister's marriage. My grandmother's dream would remain, wakeful and alive.

She dreamed of the tiny plot of land that she would tend, living off its proceeds, until her death. But her dream never came true, nor did any other dreams she had. None of them at all—even when she climbed into the Bedford truck that took her from her village to the outskirts of Muscat for an appointment with Dr. Thoms, or "Thomas" as the locals called him, the famous missionary doctor, reviving the fantasy of regaining her sight completely in the eye that the herbal remedies of the ignorant had obliterated. But Dr. Thoms reduced her dream to nothing. He told her that the pain in that eye would go away on its own but the herbal infusion that had been repeatedly applied had caused permanent loss of sight in it. No surgery that he could perform would bring it back. She had to be content with her one good eye, he said. She would have to make do. So she was content. She made do. She climbed back into the truck bed, without a word, and returned to the village.

And I . . . My sight still misty and blurred by the dream-fog I was in, the open arms she held out to me, I would sometimes forget that she had died. Getting up to look for her, I searched the corridors between rooms. I could hear my Chinese classmates arguing, and the little screams of my Nigerian neighbor having sex with a Colombian student she'd taken a liking to recently. I would find myself wandering barefoot into the ice-cold kitchen. The snow would not have stopped. Finally, remembering that she was dead, I ceased searching the corridors.

Kuhl had been trying to convince Suroor to give up her room now and then, so that she could be alone with her husband. He was living in a tiny flat with five other Pakistani men, so it was impossible for her to go there. Kuhl lived with a married relative of theirs and her husband, since their flat literally abutted the college of medicine, while the university's residence halls were quite a distance away. Even if she tried to apply for university housing now, she wouldn't be allowed to complete the paperwork and move before the end of the term. The two of them had used up all their funds on cheap hotels and B&Bs, and her father the banker was not going to increase the amount he transferred monthly to his daughters. Suroor said no at first, but finally she gave in, leaving the key for her sister and spending those hours at the university library or trying to study in the park. But it didn't get any easier, and she never did get used to the idea. She couldn't even stand the thought of it. She confided to me that it made her feel filthy. Their parents weren't stingy with anything. And here were Suroor and Kuhl, so far away, conspiring behind their backs. She couldn't stop thinking about what the pair of them were doing in her room. About that hand—that rough peasant hand—on her sister's soft, smooth throat; his coarse lips on her pampered body. This was torture, Suroor said. She couldn't stand it.

Brown Rings on a Woman's Head-Shawl

I walk through the antique streets of this city that carries so much history, my book-filled bag on my back, the laces on my trainers neatly tied. I walk through the streets, an alien here in my feelings, my gestures, my speech. As the poet al-Mutanabbi put it, "a stranger in face and hand and tongue." I am thinking about Suroor's pain, about *filthiness*, about the justifications people drum up. In the end everyone does what they want to do, and they always find ways to justify it. Their words of excuse come into existence along with the acts they validate—and it's an easy birth these excuses have.

When I'm tired of walking, I sit down at a café, a table by the window overlooking the street, and I order a black coffee. I stop worrying over Suroor and her sister and people's excuses. But I'm not really seeing this large cup or the black liquid it holds. What I see in front of me is a tiny cup filled with dark brown coffee gripped in fleshy, wrinkled fingers.

In my mind, I see the pale shadow cast by the house's outer wall onto the ground inside the compound, and I see her sitting on a mat in the courtyard, her legs stretched in front of her, absorbed in drinking her coffee. She is not weighted down by thoughts. She is not remembering anything, not missing anything or wishing for it, not dreaming of anything as she sits under the ample shade of the bitter orange tree.

The children had grown up and her lap was empty now. Her one good eye had gone dull and she could barely see; there was no needle and thread in her hand these days, no length of fabric. Her legs were infirm now and she no longer made her way from the house out to the fields in the late afternoons. She sat. That's all. She sat, drinking her coffee, nothing else; returning neighbors' greetings when the women stopped by to say hello, as they were on their way home, waving away the relentless flies, once in a while uttering a couple of words or a sentence, sipping her coffee, without any of it returning her to the past, to memory. As if nothing existed beyond this moment, beyond drinking her coffee; or as if it were an eternal moment that had always existed and always would. As if the past never happened, as if her father's justifications for throwing her out of his house, along with her brother, did not still linger somewhere inside her head. As if her brother's youth—her brother's life—had not collapsed beneath the many mud-brick walls he had built back then, receiving a paltry five bisa coins for every wall.

She sat in the gloomy shade drinking her coffee. The past was obscured now; the time when she had roasted the black-brown beans herself, and ground them by hand with her cast-iron pestle, and watched closely as the coffee began to boil in the little brass pot, lifting it off the heat at exactly the right moment. Now all she did was drag her body with its lifeless legs over the ground, from her room out to the shade of the wall in the courtyard. The Bengali would emerge from the kitchen with a thermos made in Taiwan, and a little cup, setting it all down beside her without looking at her, and then he would go away. Like us. Like all of us, we all went away, hurrying off to friends, to homework, to our little secrets, to the TV, to racing one another on our bicycles, to little quarrels in the neighborhood, while she remained there, sitting in the shade of the wall, even if she was not yet calling out, "Don't go." She conducted herself properly, suitably, as one must, understanding the justifications that people had, or not thinking much about them, self-contained, drinking her coffee.

I left the café, slinging my bag over my shoulder. The snow had started falling again, and I hugged my wool jacket closer around my body. How do our bodies find it so easy to obey clothing that they've never before learned to wear? When I was little, in the cold season she always insisted on bringing out that square green woolen shawl and knotting it around my neck. I never dared to object. In the summer, I wore whatever lightweight garments she had sewn for me, and in the winter I wrapped myself up in the shawl and breathed in the heavy, pungent smell of wool. When I started school, I changed out of the traditional clothing everyone wore in the village into my blue pinafore. And later, when I went to Muscat, I replaced my traditional village clothes with a skirt and blouse. When I traveled to this cold land, I changed out of my traditional clothes and wore a jacket and trousers instead. She never shed the clothes that were native to the village she came from. Even when her legs could no longer carry her and she had to drag herself out to the shade of the courtyard, she did not complain about her long, loose clothing getting in her way. She went on sitting there looking as she had looked, it seemed, for all eternity: in her bright-colored cotton tarha and the black tunic that fell below her knees, embroidered at the bodice, with light, colorful sleeves, and her closely fitting sirwal trousers beneath, showing their inches of fine silver embroidery around the cuffs. Never in her life had she put on an abaya, nor any garment other than these with which she had grown up. The small trunk in which she kept her clothing held a few tunics and pairs of finely worked sirwals, and nothing else. Her night clothes were simply the daytime clothes that had gotten too old, the fabric too thin to wear in daylight. There were no underclothes. Her small, carved wooden mandus held an array of little glass bottles, their colors faded, emptied of the perfumed oils they were meant to hold. That little chest also contained a silver anklet that had been her mother's, a few fine Chinese porcelain bowls, and tightly packed rows of colorful tarhas all made out of similar cotton fabric, all with repeating designs: large red roses, or green trees, or yellow stars. Running down the long edges were a few words in Swahili, stamped onto the fabric in big letters that she couldn't read, just as she couldn't read any other language. In this village where she now lived—in our village—the women called these colorful African head-shawls ghadfas or liisus, but she called them masarrs, as she had always heard them called in her own village.

When she was still a girl, and her brother could provide barely enough food for the two of them, she had yearned for a colorful headdress like all the women had. She had longed desperately for that masarr, before she learned to let go of all yearnings and the foulness they could bring in their wake.

One day, she went to the owner of the only shop in her village. She greeted him and fell silent. As she stood there, not moving, he was busying himself with his stacks of canned food and jars of samna and honey. When he spoke, his voice was very loud, as though she were hard of hearing. "What does Bint Aamir want?"

My grandmother stared with her one good eye at the

piles of dreamed-of masarrs. "I want a masarr," she said, her voice little more than a hoarse whisper. The shopkeeper sighed. "But a masarr costs two qirsh, and you're completely dependent on your brother, and all he gets are day wages." He went back to his work, now straightening the imported fabrics, soft, expensive duryahi cloth and silk from India. But she didn't go away. She just stood there. She wasn't looking at the silks but at the cotton masarrs. A few years after Bint Aamir stood in the shop, their price would dwindle to less than a quarter-qirsh each. But at that time—in the days of hunger and inflation—a masarr did cost two entire qirsh. Her fist had never once closed around such a sum of money. The shopkeeper gazed at her quizzically. "I want to buy a masarr," she said. "Bi-s-sabr, with your patience—on credit. I'll make charcoal. I'll bring you the two qirsh." It all came out in one rush of breath. Bi-s-sabr wa-basakhkhim wa-barudd lak al-qirshayn. As the words came out, no longer imprisoned inside her, she felt her chest expand with air—the chest of a girl who had barely said goodbye to childhood as she stepped into adolescence. She had never paid any notice to that chest, the slight swellings on her front, but the shop owner noticed. He gave the wood door panel a little push and suddenly the windowless shop was dark. "Come over here," the shop owner said. "You can look at the masarrs and pick one out. You're not below any of those women who have them." She came closer to him, scarcely believing he was ready to let her buy one. Both hands gripped the soft fabric, while the shop owner's gaze fixed on her chest. He was very close to her now and he gasped out, "I can show you something sweeter than that masarr." With a quick movement of his hand, there facing her, he opened the izar wrapped around his waist. She had no mother. She was poor. She had been thrown out of her father's care and protection. But she was still his daughter. She was the girl who belonged to the proud horseman whose courage the women chanted in their melodic poem-songs. For just a moment the shock of it froze her. She didn't understand what it was she was being shown. But she understood that he wanted something unacceptable from her. Something despicable. That some kind of bargain was on offer. She found some strength, retrieved some pride, as the daughter of the father who had thrown her out. "I am Bint Aamir!" she shrieked, over and over, as she threw the masarrs in his face and fled the shop.

Two days later, the shopkeeper's sister came to her door clutching a masarr that was patterned in interlacing brown rings. She entered the dilapidated room that was their home, the half-collapsed structure to which she and her brother had come seeking some kind of shelter. She unfolded the new masarr in front of Bint Aamir. "Pretty?" she asked. Her listener swallowed. The shop owner's sister went on. "Here, take it, on credit," she said. "But you have to pay back the two qirsh before the feast day."

For the first time since her mother's death, Bint Aamir felt a glimmer of joy in her life. She promised she would repay the debt before the feast day. After their goodbyes, she laid the masarr out on the mat. Her fingers traced the brown rings, around and around, one after another. She would have preferred one imprinted with red roses, but this masarr was now hers. And it was new, and the fabric was soft, even if it was covered in dullish brown rings. She was walking on clouds. Her eyes were wet as she hugged the soft fabric of her own new masarr to her face and fell asleep.

That was when she began to spend her time with the musakhkhammat—the coal-faced women, they were called, because they made and sold charcoal. Provisioning herself with dates and water, she went out with them, walking far from the village, beyond the fields, and out to the desert. They gathered dead wood all day long. At sundown, they set fire to the wood and then buried it in the sand. As the embers smoldered, they formed a circle around the hole they had dug. They waited for the wood to die, eating their dates. They spent the whole night waiting for the embers to turn to charcoal. In the predawn light, they brushed away the layer of sand, dug out the black sukhkhaam, and divided it up. Each woman tied her share in a bundle that she then hoisted onto her back and carried home before the sun was up. In the suq, a load of coal would fetch a half-qirsh. She had to go out every day for a week to amass as much as a wiqr of charcoal, enough to sell. The loads of wood frayed her thin, tattered her clothes even further. But before the feast day she had managed to acquire two silver qirsh coins.

She went out once again, though, with the charcoal women to help them and to say goodbye. She told them she would come back from time to time to make charcoal. Doing so would help her brother, even if only a little. But that night she couldn't leave them, because Umayra suddenly went into labor. The other charcoal women had to tend to her instead of their embers. Bint Aamir was left to attend to the embers as they turned into charcoal, and she was the one who gathered it all up. Just before dawn, Umayra gave birth. She wrapped her tiny, puckered baby boy in a rag and tied him over her share of the coal. She began to walk, carrying both bundles, her charcoal and her baby boy, back to the village, arriving home before the sun came up.

How to Behave Suitably

I wake up. It's still dark, and from my bed all is silent. But I was there, in that dirt space in the back courtyard of the house and I was running, and that little forgotten space was itself like some kind of misdeed, and I was chasing this feeling, of having done something wrong. I was there by myself, running. She wasn't in my dream. It was a dream of the place, of the childhood misdeed that place meant. No, she wasn't there. Where had she gone, and how had she left my dreams? Why was she no longer stretching out her arms, and why weren't her wrinkles forming little smiles, smiling at me? Where was the civet musk I always smelled? Maybe she had just gone out for a little while. Gone out of my dreams just long enough to take home our neighbor Shaykha, who was out of her mind and had gone wandering outside again without putting her sirwal on. Or perhaps she had left my dream just long enough to grab my little brother, Sufyan, by the underarms and pitch him high and catch him again, as she sang out a mother's rhyme, again and again. *Misk wi-zbbaad wi-uud wi-hall, tammayt sanatayn la adhan wa-la akhal... Musk and civet essence and aloeswood and oil: Two years with my baby, no call for tinctures or kohl!* Or maybe she had walked out of my dreams to go and pay her respects to the Tomb of the Prophet, which she had dreamed of visiting but never could. Or perhaps to line her one sound eye with kohl, though her eyesight was now too weak even in that one working eye to see what she was doing. Whatever it was, she had walked out of my dreams and she hadn't come back. She was no longer there.

I no longer shouted those words in my sleep: "Don't go!" She no longer smiled tenderly as she buried me in her embrace. She had gone. She abandoned me. She left me behind, thinking backward through the succession of time: winter snow, autumn, summer, spring... and all that time, she didn't come back, not even once. Maybe she had not forgiven me? Maybe she had grown tired of trying to interpret the excuses that people made for themselves? Maybe, probably, she decided to leave us once and for all to our little occupations, our oblivious bustle. She decided to retract those words, *Don't go*, to return them to the place from which she had launched them. Maybe she did have in her grip those thin and magic threads that pull words back from the consequences they bring and return them to where they first form inside us. Maybe she gathered up all the *Don't gos*, those we said to her and those she said to us. She spooled them in to where they belonged and kept them there. Most likely she'd had enough of forgiving the sins and faults of the world.

I was in the dark, in a bed that was mine for now, in a foreign land. My spirit was burning, consumed by my human helplessness, the impossibility of regaining or restoring just one moment from the past. I was asking only for one single moment, no more, but even that was impossible. All I wanted was to make one little swerve, to take just one step back: and then, from there, I would not *go away*. Her hair, which she always treated so carefully, applying oil and combing and braiding it. Her hair, which scissors never touched, had gone bunched and frizzy around her face and shoulders. It had become intensely, purely white, pure like the truth. She had gotten very thin, as the flesh clinging to her tall frame seemed to melt away. Her fingernails, neglected now, were no longer encased in what had been the full, strong flesh of those fingers I remembered. Her eye could barely make out the shadow outlines of people, and her mouth was almost incapable of taking in food of any sort. Going into her room, I had to hold my breath, trying to fend off the stench of urine, before greeting her in a brisk voice loud enough that she could hear me.

"Zuhour! Zuhour," she would rasp, "I want some rice." I would tell her I had brought some. But she couldn't chew it. I fled from the odor, from the grains clinging to the sides of her mouth, from the black nail beneath which dirt had collected. I fled as she was calling out. "Zuhoooouur . . . don't go. Stay with me a bit, just a little. I want someone here with me, don't go." But I would go. No. This moment, this one moment, would not come back, no matter how hard I begged it to return. I would go. "Zuhoooouur . . . Zuhour." Maybe I was not truly *Zuhour*; how could I have a name that meant "pretty blossoms," when now I was someone who did not even turn around, or pay any attention? She called and called, for an entire month. "Don't go away, don't anybody go away, stay with me." We didn't stay: not me, not my brother, Sufyan, nor my sister, Sumayya. We all fled from her messy white hair and her stench. From her unsuitable behavior, her inappropriate looks and smells, her calling out, those sounds that disobeyed the old, old boundaries of the way one ought to be—where whatever one was offered, one felt thankful for, favorably treated, and nothing further was asked.

I would walk through the city, and sit in lecture halls, and eat cold sandwiches in the cafeteria, and drink tea with Suroor in the kitchen in our university housing block. But there was a blindfold over my eyes. I couldn't see anything. I didn't know why that was, or what it was that I could not see. I could feel the blindfold, and I could sense my unseeingness, but I couldn't understand anything.

Finally, Suroor had confronted her sister. "For how long

did you contract this mutaa marriage? A month? Two? My patience has run out." But her sister responded with calm assurance. "The contract is six months, but we are going to make it permanent. We were made for each other."

Suroor came to me. "She says they were made for each other, Zuhour. No one is created just for someone else. And especially, no illiterate peasant from the lowest of the low is created for a refined, soft-skinned, pale-complexioned princess! But she says she means to make their marriage permanent. My father will just die if he finds out." Yes, Suroor was very pretty, but she was not created for passion, and she would never be in love. The blindfold over her eyes was thick indeed, and she did not see.

Bint Aamir wrapped the brown-ringed masarr around her head and knotted the two qirsh coins at one end, and went to the shop. She found it closed. Some boys who were tossing around a handmade cloth ball told her that the shop owner was at home. He was dying. She went to the house and his sister let her into his room. It was as dark as his shop, and the smell of the olive oil, black pepper, and clove mixture they had rubbed into his skin could stop one's breath cold. She saw his wife sitting at his feet, her eyes red. He was panting and rasping as if trying to get a bit of air. The mutawwib was standing at his head. "Say: I ask God's forgiveness for all my sins, the trivial ones and the important ones, the open and the hidden, the small and the vast, the ones I know and the ones I don't know." The shop owner did not say a word. He simply coughed and moaned hoarsely and leaned toward the cup of water in his wife's grip.

She came into the room and walked firmly over to his bed. She spoke in a very loud voice, as though he were hard of hearing. "I am Bint Aamir, and I have come to repay my debt, for the masarr I took on credit." The hoarse breathing stopped and he stared in her direction. She undid the knot at the end of her masarr and took out the two big silver coins. He put out a thin, weak-looking hand and closed it around the money. His fingers trembled and his rasping resumed. The mutawwib ordered, "Forgive her debt, give her back the two qirsh." But the shop owner's fist tightened around the coins, and then he pushed them under his pillow. She left his room. She walked out of his house. Now the masarr was hers. She had freed herself.

Mud and Charcoal

Suroor and I were in the library. I was helping her read a manuscript in Arabic. She was telling me how much she wanted to improve her Urdu, too—her "second language," as it was considered suitably and properly to be by the petite bourgeoisie of Pakistan. She was trying to concentrate on the text, although in reality she couldn't focus her thoughts on anything but her sister, Kuhl. But was this person truly her sister? Suroor felt like she hardly knew her anymore. Kuhl's emotions were always fraught and her mind was elsewhere. She was walking through life on a frothy cloud, she was caught in a waiting game, she was only passing by, or crossing through. Not really *living*. She would tell Suroor that her soul was suspended on the ripply little folds between the buttons on her beloved's shirt. That her spirit hung helplessly there, bumping against the pleats and creases and wrinkles of his shirt. This passion—everything about this consuming love!—Suroor simply could not understand or accept it. How could the spirit of any creature be pledged like this, to the creases of a shirt and its buttons? How could anyone mortgage their soul away? She didn't understand the story of the shirt at all. How could those ordinary wrinkles that form on any shirt when one sits down be—on the shirt of one particular person—a snare that caught the soul in its creases?

Suddenly she stopped reading. "But you didn't tell me," she said. "You never told me you had a grandmother."

"Everyone has grandmothers," I said.

She laughed. She was so innocent. "Of course, everyone has grandmothers. But your family—they are well off, aren't they? So why ... why would your grandmother wish she could be a peasant farmer?"

"Maybe she was like the wife of Mu'tamid bin Abbad," I replied. "The wife could see the peasant women from the balcony of her palace, and she longed to walk barefoot on the soil as they did. So her husband, the emir, thought the only thing to do was to bedeck the courtyard of the palace with perfume, saffron, musk, and camphor, and he ordered that it all be anointed with water until it was as damp as the soil in the fields. His wife went out to stroll with her daughters and her attendants, plunging her feet into the perfumed soil just as the peasant women did in the real soil." Just then Suroor's phone rang and she was immediately plunged into conversation with her sister. I left the library.

It was just a funny story. I had no wish to scratch up Suroor's pure innocence. Suroor seemed to me like a porcelain figurine, while my grandmother was a mountain. After my grandmother's brother died, she found herself alone in the half-ruined shack where they lived with two minute coffee cups, a small platter, a cooking pot, two bedsheets, some worn-out clothes, and a new head wrap imprinted with brown rings. She learned from women in the neighborhood that some man had presented himself as a marriage prospect but her father had refused to allow her to wed. She went back to working with the charcoal women. Many, many years ago, Mu'tamid bin Abbad said, "They will be walking in the soil, their feet bare, as if what their feet touch is not musk and camphor." As for my grandmother and her charcoal-making friends, all they knew of camphor and musk were the words.

One day she fainted while they were on their way back to the village. The charcoal she was carrying on her back scattered across the ground. The women gathered it up, but they had a much harder time trying to rouse her. The sun had already come up; at home, their waking husbands and children found no one baking their bread. The women dragged her, half-conscious, all the way to her shack. She would follow her brother before long, they whispered to each other. But in fact, she would live to see eighty.

It was on that day, late in the afternoon, that Salman and his wife, Athurayyaa, came to visit. Salman was a relative on her mother's side. After her brother's death, he had invited her to live in his household but she had refused. Two years passed, and her health was deteriorating. This time, he came with his wife to take her away. He helped her pack the pitcher, the two tiny cups, the cooking pot, the platter, and the two sheets. She wound her new masarr about her head and neck, put on her silver anklet, and went away with them.

My grandmother never did own her own little plot of land to till. She lived for eighty years, or perhaps it was longer, and she died before she came to own anything on the face of this earth. She had a green thumb: it was she who planted all the lemon and bitter orange trees in the courtyard of our house. One bitter orange tree was her favorite, but no tree that she planted and tended had ever withered. But still, it was our house, our courtyard, our trees. She lived with us, that's all. She didn't own the building, or the land, or even us. I think of her as my grandmother, but we weren't really her grandchildren.

She would lean her back against the bitter orange tree, and stretch her legs out in front of her, and cuddle my infant brother and sing to him.

> _Ya hooba hooba hooba, ya hooba wana_
> _uhibbuh,_
> _wahibb illi yuhibbuh,_
> _wa-ʿasr ana mrawwahat buh an al-_
> _ghashshun tihib-bu,_

willi yibba habibi yibii' ummuh wabuuh,
wiybii' khiyaar maluh min il-mabsali
  wakhuuh,

ya hooba hooba hooba . . . until my brother went to sleep.
On and on it went, over and over.

Hooba hooba I love this little one,
I love anyone who loves this baby son
In the late afternoon I hold him oh so tight
sheltered from the wind gusts mighty or
  slight
Anyone who wants him, will they sell their
  ma and pop
Anyone who wants him, will they sell their
  fine date crop . . .

She always made a little bed for him in the shade of the
narinjah tree, smoothing out his hair as he slept. That's where
she would work the dried lemons, taking out the darkened
inner flesh, which she used to make broth, and then boiling
the hardened brown peel to make the infusion that calmed
my mother's spells of nausea during her frequent pregnancies. In the clear, peaceful late afternoons, she sat with her
old neighbor Shaykha, before the dementia got to her. They

drank coffee and ate dates and talked. What did they talk about? There's no doubt that the only subject Shaykha talked about was her son, whom I never saw. Even when I first met Shaykha—she was already an old woman then—her son had grown up and gone very far away. He was very far away; he was very emigrant. I don't remember what my grandmother ever talked about. My little brother Sufyan's crying, or perhaps his irritation at having to drink baby formula? The new fruit growing on the narinjah tree? The only trip she ever made with us, when we went to the Emirates? An accursed hump on the back of a woman named Rayya? Or did she ever talk about the one man who had offered his hand in marriage, and was refused by her father?

The Widow Marries

When life in the village began stifling Salman, and he felt he couldn't make a living there, he traveled to Zanzibar. He was not yet twenty. He borrowed money and bought a little farm and planted trees: banana, mango, coconut, clove. Soon he was able to begin marketing the harvest. In only a few years, he had amassed savings enough that not only could he pay off his loan, but he could return to Oman, buy and furnish a house, and think about getting married. But he preferred to stay in Zanzibar, moving among his slave mistresses, his farm, and his commerce. It was a family tragedy that forced him to return to Oman to care for his mother and sisters. And so he was in his late twenties when he became engaged to his paternal cousin Athurayyaa, widowed by her second husband at the age of sixteen.

Athurayyaa had been a little girl, barely completing her fifth year of life, when her cousin Salman left for Zanzibar. She didn't have any memory of him, didn't recognize him when he returned, even if his name was a familiar one in her father's house. As a two-time widow, she had gotten a reputation for being ill-omened. People whispered that anyone who married her would surely die. And so Athurayyaa did not expect to marry a third time. Her first husband had betrothed her when she was nine and had consummated the marriage when she was eleven. He was in his late sixties. At the time, she was still in braids and going out to play in the alleyways with other girls. They gathered sticks and string and remnants of fabric to make dolls. They drew lines and squares for playing hopscotch and took turns hopping from one space to the next. Her mother-in-law had to drag her in before sunset, hide her wood-and-fabric dolls, and bathe her, transforming her into a woman for nightfall. Athurayyaa was afraid of her husband. She didn't understand at all why he did what he did to her every night, and why she couldn't play with her friends when he was around. When he grew ill and died she was delighted because that meant her mother-in-law would no longer hide her dolls and scold her for getting her clothes dirty. But the joy was short-lived. Her mother-in-law pulled off her bright-colored gown and dressed her in white mourning clothes. The woman draped her long braids in a black tarha just as she draped all the mirrors in the house in black. The woman told her she had to stay inside, exactly like this, in these clothes, and that she would not leave the house for four months and ten days. Athurayyaa wailed and writhed on the floor, and the women who came to mourn with them bent over her in concern. "Ma sha Allah! So young, but she knows her duty and weeps for her man." Two years later, another man secured her hand in marriage. He wasn't so elderly but he was crude and rough and had no sense of how things ought to be. He was a hunter and he couldn't be tamed. He would go off alone on his hunting expeditions. She was sixteen and pregnant for the first time when a group of Bedouin showed up carrying her husband, torn to pieces by wolves in the desert. She put on mourning white again and gave birth to a baby who had died in her womb.

When Salman saw her, he was smitten with the look in her eyes. It was the expression of someone who had experienced everything, who knew everything, and therefore no longer took any interest in the world. It was a look both careworn and uncaring. The self-sufficiency and superiority in that look could make you dizzy. It was the look of a little girl who had already become a mother—and of a mother whose dolls had been hidden from her and whose newborn baby had been buried. Salman liked Athurayyaa's nose, too. Trying to persuade his mother to betroth him to her, he described her nose as being as fine as a sharp sword. He loved her almond mouth, her long hands that looked as free and innocent as a child's, untouched by hard work; hands that had the appearance of never having rubbed the rough skin of her geriatric first husband or held the torn flesh that had once been her hunter husband. Hands that surely never held a baby except to lower it into its grave. It was as though those hands had been created for his hands alone: to enclose his fingers, and muss his hair. He would eat out of her hand all his life and he would never feel that he had enough. This hand would hold him and shade him and guide him and protect him. Her hand, the hand of his cousin Athurayyaa. So what if she was a widow. So what if she had borne a baby that had died. He didn't want anyone else. No substitute would ever satisfy him.

At the wedding, Athurayyaa felt uncomfortable and embarrassed. She felt shame. Marriage was beyond her now, she thought; suddenly, she felt so very old. Even if Salman was ten years her senior, to her he seemed a callow youth. All through the festivities, as they went on and on, she felt awkward and confused. But she did sense from the start that Salman was enraptured by her, and for the first time in her life she did come to know a man's love. And because of that, she knew that any child she had with him would live, and that is exactly what happened.

Ten months later, Athurayyaa gave birth to a beautiful

baby girl, healthy and strong. Salman named her Hasina, and she held all those around her in perfect thrall. She lived in the bliss of her playful days until, years later, the journey of life gave her a new script to follow.

An Austere Party for the Passionately Ascetic

Christine invited us to a party at her house. It turned out to be a disappointment, because Christine—the unbending vegan—did not allow any animal products, no milk, no eggs, into her home. And so there was nothing to eat but potato chips, and a strange kind of cake that didn't contain any milk or egg. Some of the guests—we were all students—perched on high metal stools without cushions or backs in the crowded kitchen and began talking to one another about their studies and what they had to read next and their professors. More guests were standing in the hall or the sitting room, exchanging similar conversations, the endlessly repeated chatter of students. I said to Suroor, "We are going to die of boredom even before we die of hunger."

There was nothing really to look at in Christine's simple apartment; her home seemed a reflection of Christine's own unadorned self. She was constantly on the move. Today she wore a green T-shirt on which was printed FRIENDS OF THE EARTH, and jeans and running shoes. She was unusually tall, so tall that people had to tip their faces upward to address her. Her hands always seemed to be darting about, her fingers going up unconsciously to toy with the tiny silver ring in her nose. It was impossible to avoid noticing the tattooed cross on her wrist that she had gotten when she was sixteen years old. Her very pale blond hair was always gathered in a ponytail, and if she wasn't wearing the green T-shirt, then she would certainly be wearing a blue one that was otherwise identical. Her cup of decaf coffee with soy milk was tall and skinny: it looked just like her. Here at this party, she was an exact scan of the figure I always saw at the university: T-shirt jeans running shoes ponytail nose ring tattoo long skinny cup. The only difference was that, at home, she didn't have her gray Adidas backpack over her shoulders.

My Arab colleagues were applying themselves energetically to the whiskey bottles that these young men had brought with them. Kuhl had gone into the apartment's one bedroom to be by herself with her phone. Christine shared this apartment with a classmate from China. In the narrow corridor stood Suroor, her slender fingers clutching a glass of juice, the perfectly manicured nails visible. She was having an intense discussion with two male students, one Norwegian and the other Korean, about hijab. Standing around like this didn't appeal to me, and I was beginning to feel tired as well as bored. I swooped down on Kuhl in the bedroom. My timing was lucky: she was no longer on her phone.

She was wiping her eyes on a tissue. I felt embarrassed, and I am sure it showed. But she made room for me on the bed where she was already sitting.

"Suroor has told you everything, right?" she asked me after a moment.

I was hesitant; I didn't know what to say. She went on. "Suroor doesn't understand anything. She thinks she does, but in fact she doesn't understand anything at all."

I couldn't find any words. So I occupied myself by staring at each wall in turn. There was nothing to look at except a photograph of Christine's father, who was a professor of mathematics at Columbia University, and a small map of New York. "Christine's from New York," I said. My voice came out flat and dull.

"That's what she always says," replied Kuhl. Something in the tone of her voice made me instantly aware that she was older than Suroor. Maybe more mature, as well. Her eyes were close to my face. They weren't focusing on anything around her, and I felt her nearness, as I noticed the determination those eyes seemed to hold. She began scraping her fingers across the pillow; her nails were a rose color. She was definitely a bit fuller than Suroor, her features less well defined. Suddenly I had an inkling: her family must have always been fixated on this difference in appearance—in attractiveness—between the two sisters, and this preoccupation must have conveyed to Kuhl unconsciously that she did not deserve the best. It was a disturbing thought. I began staring at the walls again. There was nothing up there to suggest the presence of Christine's Chinese flatmate.

Kuhl spoke suddenly. "I cherish my parents," she said. "I really do hold them in very high esteem, believe me. I respect the family name, I respect— Suroor doesn't understand. She thinks that by marrying Imran I am betraying my family. But she doesn't underst—"

"Don't apologize, Kuhl."

"Was I apologizing?" She sounded startled. "Yes, all right, you have a point, I'm always apologizing. Suroor—"

I interrupted her again. "This attachment you have, this kind of feeling—what greater justification could there be, anyway?"

The tears glistened in her eyes. "It isn't just that Imran is right for me. And suitable. He completes me. I was only half a person before I found him. Our comfort together, how good we feel, the strength of our love—it can't be put into words."

Suddenly she started crying, her whole body trembling. I put my arm around her shoulder. "Don't cry, Kuhl. It's your choice, and you are perfectly capable of making good choices."

Her voice came unevenly, broken up by her sobs. "But I didn't choose anything. This was not about making a choice. Suroor simply does not understand. I don't want to wrong anyone, and I don't want to reduce Suroor's chances of finding an appropriate husband from a distinguished family, but . . . but, Imran . . ."

She wiped her tears dry on a tissue and suddenly her face was radiant and her voice was sure. "Imran—when I wake up early in the morning and find that I'm not in his arms, I feel like my existence has no meaning at all."

Suddenly, Christine appeared in the doorway. Seeing us, she raised her thin eyebrows. "Were you investigating my clothes closet?" she asked lightly.

Kuhl laughed. "And what would we find there, besides blue and green Friends of the Earth T-shirts?"

I heard Christine's loud laughter. I could never understand how a body that thin could emit such a powerful laugh. It was late, and I made my excuses and said my goodbyes.

In the following months I saw a lot of Kuhl, when she wasn't busy with her studies or with Imran. We went for long walks in the public gardens. She talked incessantly, as if she had just discovered language. I loved listening to her—to that impeccable upper-class British accent, which she had acquired from her British teachers in primary school, and her unexpected little intakes of breath between sentences. For me, Kuhl crafted a world of words, and she wanted to bring me inside it. For a moment, I imagined myself a part of it. But in reality, I wasn't a part of anything at all.

The Bride, and the Baby Repelled

My grandmother went home with her relative Salman and his wife, Athurayya, and she stayed for forty years.

When her brother died and Salman first invited her to live under his protection and care, she had already heard talk that his circumstances were in disarray. The dates he cultivated on his land were his main source of income. Sultan Saʻid bin Taymur's government in Muscat had increased taxes fourfold on all dates exported through the port of Sur. And so Bint Aamir stayed where she was, determined not to accept his offer. But the constant exertion of turning wood into charcoal was depleting her strength. And anyway, people were saying that the British had surely intervened to lower the taxes on dates, fearing that the imam and his supporters in the country's interior would harness popular discontent over taxes to foment a rebellion against the sultan, London's ally.

Salman and Athurayya's only daughter, Hasina, was ten years old at the time. Her eyes blazed with an energy and a readiness that did not shrink from the unknown world of her future. Her body was developing rapidly, and the still-hidden contours of womanhood would soon appear. She showed no emotion toward the new guest in their home, so Bint Aamir mostly ignored her, occupying herself with the household's daily tasks. Only a few years remained before the girl-child grew enough that she could become a bride, before she would leave the household behind.

My grandmother watched closely as Hasina was transformed into a bride, overseeing the details. Hasina bundled up the new silk gowns and packed the fine china and the worked silver anklets, the silver pendants and the gold earrings, and the incense chest. Not yet fifteen, Hasina went away with her husband, first to Algeciras and then to Burundi, where before much time had passed, all news of her ceased abruptly. She sent two or three letters to her parents, assuring them that she and her new husband had settled in well, and that her husband had bought a farm, and then that she had given birth to twins. And then, silence. No one heard anything at all of Hasina until the mid-1980s when her grandsons returned, to seek Omani citizenship. Their request was rejected.

In Salman's house, the years passed peacefully. He engrossed himself in his shop and his farmland. Meanwhile, the camaraderie grew between his wife, Athurayyaa, and his guest, Bint Aamir. Just as it seemed to all of them that nothing would ever disturb the world again, the terrible impact of the Second World War seemed to create an impasse before them that would never be overcome. Life in Zanzibar had taught Salman what he had to do, had given him the key that alone might unlock some income. Take a risk; try something new. He ventured to Bombay, seeking to expand his commercial ties. He came back with only meager profits but he found something more profound in its consequences. In Bombay, he encountered Sulaiman al-Baruni, the sultan of Muscat's advisor for religious affairs. Al-Baruni's illness—which would be fatal—did not prevent him from urging Salman to explore India's flourishing trade in Arabic publishing, and to do so with gusto. This turned out to be Salman's most valuable booty from the voyage, and it would change Athurayyaa's life forever.

Now Salman made use of his leisure time at the shop to read *al-Azhar al-riyadiyya fi a'imma wa-muluk al-ibadiyya*, the copy that al-Baruni had dedicated to him, with a signature in his own hand. As he immersed himself in this classic work on the history of his Ibadi Muslim faith's imams and rulers, Athurayyaa—who had learned to read as a little girl at her local mosque school—devoted her time to other books that had been issued by the presses of Calcutta and Hyderabad. She all but memorized *Stories of the Prophets* and *The*

Correct Word on the Prophet's Companions. What particularly moved her were the lives of the prophets and the pious, and her reading dislodged the sure contentment that had always governed her quiet, peaceful, earthly life. With tears running down her face, she recounted to Bint Aamir the story of the Prophet Muhammad's Companion whose foot was amputated as he was praying, and he did not even feel it. She grieved for the fact that she would never attain such a rarefied pitch of pious observance and devout humility. But a mysterious light had been lit inside of her. Following its steady guidance extinguished her worldly concerns, which now appeared so inconsequential in the glow of that inner flame. All through her thirties, she immersed herself in attempts to reach this new and compelling goal—to arrive at the wellsprings of this holy light.

And then, as Athurayyaa approached forty years of age and her husband turned fifty and was preparing himself to make the sacred pilgrimage to Mecca—a crowning touch to the life of a prosperous merchant, which would seal the goodness by which he had tried to live with a pious act—she woke up one morning to discover that she was pregnant. She, a grandmother whose grandsons were already old enough to be working in a farm somewhere in Burundi! Athurayyaa was dismayed. She was embarrassed. Mortified. But Salman saw her pregnancy as a good omen. His world still looked vast and full of promise. He postponed his intended pilgrimage, and joyously prepared to receive his new child.

Athurayyaa had a difficult labor. Salman all but destroyed the midwife's door, trying to get her to come back with him just after midnight to save his wife and the unborn baby. Two days went by before the baby emerged, feet first. The midwife brought the newborn close to Athurayyaa's perspiring face. She found him an ugly sight, and she turned her head away. She refused to open her arms to him. She would not pick him up, would not nurse him. The neighbor women said among themselves, "Athurayyaa can't stand the sight of her baby boy, she's rejected him completely."

Her husband bought one ewe after another. They squeezed the milk from those thin teats into large conch shells that had horns slender enough for the baby to take into his mouth. But the milk wasn't enough for him, and he cried day and night.

My grandmother—ten years younger than Athurayyaa—surmised that her friend was in the grip of the madness that strikes some women as they sweat through the terrors of childbirth. She gathered the baby into her own embrace. And so then the women were whispering among themselves the news that Bint Aamir—who had never married, had never once given birth—had found milk gushing from her own breasts for Athurayyaa's newborn. In fact, they murmured, her milk was so abundant that she had to release the excess flow into the packed dirt of the courtyard once the baby had his fill. Soon, they were telling each other that Salman was no longer buying nursing ewes for his son, not since Bint Aamir held the infant to her own body and wouldn't let go of him. As for my grandmother, she said nothing. In her embrace the baby flourished. He grew pink with health, and the spells of fever and crying stopped. Salman named the boy Salih, but my grandmother protested that this was a heavy name for a baby. His stars and this name were not in harmony, she declared. It must be changed. Still astonished at how fully the baby had taken to her, Salman tried to negotiate. She named him Mansour. "Helped by God."

About eight months later, Athurayyaa came out of the state she'd been in since the baby's birth. My grandmother just laughed when she heard us say solemnly that what our real grandmother had suffered from was *postpartum depression*. Our real grandmother, whom we never saw and never knew, since she died in her early fifties, grief-stricken at her husband's death less than a year before.

At the word *depression*, the woman I call my grandmother, Bint Aamir, simply laughed. Again she told us the story of Athurayyaa's madness and how she could not stand the sight of her son.

Even after she recovered and accepted her son, Mansour,

Athurayyaa did not intervene to alter the course of events. My father grew up believing he had two mothers and one father, exactly as we grew up later on, believing we had two mothers: my mother, who was always submerged in her sorrows and the pain of her many miscarriages, and my grandmother, always submerged in the little details of our lives and our upbringing.

Life Is a Paper Kite

Suroor's sister, Kuhl, grew up with plentiful money and a severely restricted life. She was not permitted to wear any shoes other than Clarks, with their plain, low, boxy heels, and she could not wear any customary Punjabi ensemble unless it had been sewn by the family's tailor, whose father had been their grandmother's tailor. When she made the decision, along with Suroor, to begin wearing hijab, her mother was so mortified that she concealed this development, and her daughters, from their relations—these were women, after all, who traveled regularly to London to have their hair tinted, cut, and styled. Kuhl went to an English school in Karachi, and when she graduated her father sent her to England to study medicine without seeking her opinion on the matter. Kuhl grew up on the understanding that choices in life had been assigned in advance. That her body, just as it docilely wore what she was instructed to wear—always the proper and suitable thing—would be docilely taken by the man whom someone would deem most suitable for that suitably garbed body. It never occurred to her then, not even in her deepest imaginings, that her body might have its own desires about when and how it was taken. Certainly, she never imagined that her body would demand to be taken precisely by someone *improper*; by the man who was not deemed *suitable* at all.

The first time she saw Imran he was bent over a plate of biryani in the mosque cafeteria, eating with his hand. Kuhl watched as he finished and licked his fingers; to her surprise, she felt no disgust or embarrassment at all—just a light tremor in her legs. Still, a long time had to pass before she was able to realize that in that very first moment, her desire for him had been kindled.

Her life was like a paper kite. She would lift her head to watch as it went bobbing by, the breeze taking it farther and farther away. In the beginning, she believed that she had a firm hold on the cord that tethered that kite, and that she could control its movements. But the kite didn't respond to her tugs. It flew away, eluding the pull of that thin and frail thread, which was really no more than an imaginary line. It was a kite far in the distance, hovering, circling, now ramming into a lamppost, now getting caught on an antenna, and finally, likely to be ripped to tatters as it chafed against a length of barbed wire. Or it might career back to earth, but then it would surely plunge straight into the dirt.

She asked herself why all the people around her seemed

to be holding fast to the lines that controlled their own paper kites. Their own lives. Were they knowingly creating an illusion, or were they genuinely hoping to maintain their grasp? Why was every human being granted the line that secured their kite, even though the strength of a person's grip on that cord could vary from weak to strong? Her own grip had been rubbed raw by the string that anchored her, wounding her badly enough that she let it slip out of her hand.

Suroor, for her part, was feeling more tethered. Finally, she was able to rid herself of feeling *filthy* and shake off the heavy burden of concealing her sister's love affair, for Kuhl had apparently made the decision to tell her parents and make her marriage official, public, and permanent. Suroor would perhaps no longer have to give up her room to the lovers, spending her time imagining what they were doing in her narrow, innocent little bed.

Names

Salih, who became Mansour, and would become my father, was born not long after the end of the Second World War. A new wave of inflation was sweeping across the country. Once again, flocks of emigrants were seeking meager incomes somewhere out there, at the ends of the wide world. His father, Salman, had lost all of his property except the shop and the little orchard. The child whose mother had found him so repugnant did not stop crying and screaming until Bint Aamir took him under her wing and gave him his new name. She sewed every one of his dishdashas with her own hands, through all the years until he grew up and became a man and got married. She took out portions from her rice at the midday meal and bread in the evening to supplement his share, even after easier circumstances returned to the family. By then, Salman was no longer personally locking up the huge metal chest that held the large sack of rice, the bags of flour, and the boxes of sugar, coffee, and tea. He had previously kept the key in his pocket and would open the chest for Bint Aamir before every meal, weighing out the measure of rice and flour that she would boil and bake, mid-day and evening.

Salman called her Bint Aamir, as did Athurayyaa and the neighbor women. Mansour called her Maah. That's what we children called her, too. Through those many years of her long life spent in the house of Salman, and regardless of whether it was a time of prosperity or one of the intervals of hardship between easier times, she never stopped serving the family, working in the kitchen and all through the house. It was as though, at some early moment, what lodged at the base of her conscience was the conviction that only in this way could she repay the debt she believed she owed to this household for hosting her. She never forgot for an instant that this was not her house. She never overlooked or tried to ignore her status as guest, even if in reality she was shouldering all the household tasks and raising the family's child. Her energy never flagged, so intent was she about assuring that her status in this family was deserved because of the service she gave, that it wasn't bestowed as a favor or based only on the kind charity of others.

Did Mansour bring joy to her days? Every day at dawn he would toddle along behind her, as she balanced the rotund clay jahla on her head and walked to what was known as the Shariia, the main spring at the falaj, to fill it with water. Mansour always immersed his little feet in the falaj, plunging them into the irrigation canal to make little whirl-pools. And then, on the way back, he did his solemn best to keep up with her long strides as he followed her tall figure. The early morning dew clung to his braids, which she plaited painstakingly every day until he turned twelve. Twelve years of life, through which he had managed to escape the perils of some unknown person's malicious envy. But then his father took him by the arm, shaved off his hair, and said to him, "You've become a man now, Mansour. In a few years' time, we will go on the Holy Pilgrimage together."

Mansour didn't seem to care much about having his hair cut. He didn't have dreams about going on pilgrimage to Mecca, and as it turned out, he never would perform the hajj with his father. For Salman died a very few years later, a for-eigner in Bombay, and was buried there, having traveled to the city this time seeking treatment for a constriction in his chest that was affecting his breathing.

His head shaven, Mansour immediately went back out into the nearby lanes to resume his ongoing performances for his friends. He had made it his specialty to hunt down scorpions, and once he had a heap of them, he bared his arms to create a couple of scorpion highways, while the other boys clapped and whistled. No scorpion had ever stung Mansour. Word spread among the boys that his mother Bint Aamir had drowned a scorpion in her breast milk when she was nursing him, and from that day on, no scorpion ever dared harm him. Others said she had scored and slit his arm lengthwise, sprinkled dried powdered scorpion along the incision, and sewed it up. And that was the real reason why the scorpions left him safe and sound.

Athurayyaa devoted her time entirely to prayer and acts of piety. She immersed herself in learning the Qur'an by heart, and performed extra prayers, praying and reciting from the Qur'an through the night. Meanwhile, Bint Aamir rose early every morning to take care of the needs of the household.

In Mansour's first two years, he had an occasional habit of urinating into the soft dirt of the courtyard. This would leave Athurayyaa in anguish. That was her preferred spot for performing the dawn prayers, and Mansour had made it impure. It was her favorite corner for sitting with the neighborhood women in the late morning, and Mansour had soiled it. Bint Aamir would have to fetch a trowel and remove all the soiled dirt, creating a shallow depression which she filled with fresh, pure soil. Then she took Mansour to the falaj to bathe him. She pinched his ear to remind him that he must call her whenever he needed to pee, so that she could take him to the toilet. It was called the toilet but it was nothing more than a cramped little mud-brick shelter at the end of the house, with a lengthwise split in the ground where one did one's business, and a tin pitcher for washing oneself.

Bint Aamir filled the pitcher regularly from the little falaj that passed just south of the courtyard before completing its course toward the neighbors' homes. That falaj then poured its waters into the date-palm orchards according to a strict, tightly regulated timing system based on the movement of the sun, as determined by the big sundial erected at a central location in the orchards and fields, since it was for everyone's use.

Every few months, the shamis came to empty the sewer that formed in the basin at the bottom end of the toilet slit. He charged one qirsh for his services. People had gotten into the habit of calling him the Sewer Stool Man. Mansour called him that only once. His mother Athurayyaa heard him say it. She emptied a horn of hot peppercorns onto his tongue, to teach him never to call anyone by an insulting nickname, ever again.

The Virgin

It was dark. I was floating in a spectral wave between sleep and wakefulness when I was awakened by the Nigerian girl's screams.

It was a recurring ritual that annoyed some of the students, though most didn't care. The worst thing that happened to her in response was when a student, who had already been threatened with expulsion from the university if he did not pass the end-of-year exams, broke down her door and attacked her and the guy who was with her in the room. They were naked, utterly bewildered and shaking in terror, until the student blurted out that he needed to concentrate on his studies, and that she was no longer in the jungles of her home country, and that she had better figure out how to quiet down. It was said that she made a formal complaint about his racist behavior, but it was also said that she agreed to remain silent if he paid for repairs to the door he had smashed open.

I couldn't go back inside my apparitions. My grandmother's face filled the darkness and lit it with a sallow glow. That mouth—could it ever have been a young person's mouth? I only ever saw her in old age. No one had taken a photo of her before the wrinkles began to show. Wrinkles around her mouth, carved by the drudgery of her life. Wrinkles that arrived before any man's finger or mouth could touch the soft skin of a young woman. Lips that went dry before they could be met by the lips of a lover or a husband. A face that drooped, its freshness gone, before any one man on the face of the earth could savor it. No young admirer ever gazed into that one good eye of a young woman, and saw the intelligence, determination, and magic in her gaze. No finger quivering with desire ever traced the path of her eyebrows before they turned to white. No man was ever there to put his hand out, trembling, hesitant, to her hair, to part it or to lift its locks or to inhale its beauty. She carried herself tall like a date palm or a stallion, and then she withered like an ancient tree, unseen by human eyes and untended by human hands, other than those of the physicians who pushed the sleeves up her shriveled arm abruptly to plunge their needles into the thin flesh, and those of the women who washed the dead, who stripped the clothes off this octogenarian body, the virgin body of my grandmother, before sending it, cleansed, to the grave.

Those long legs, how many times my siblings and I slept cuddled on the lap they made. How many times we played around and between them, and swung on them, and how much of our childhood filth those legs bore, before dragging us to the toilet for training as they had dragged our father years before. Legs that we so often hid behind, trying to conceal ourselves from my father's whippings and my mother's loud calls. Yes, how often we scuttled behind them to avoid a lashing that fell across her legs instead of ours, or a scolding that confronted her rather than us. Her legs never learned any other love but ours; never had a chance to give themselves to anyone but these little ones; were never desired by a man and never possessed by anyone other than us, the possessive children.

This chest against which we slept, all of us, until we were quite grown up—did it really nurse our father? It was just beginning to bud when the shop owner noticed it, and it came into full flower as the true home of our father, and then it was ours. And then it collapsed, it wilted, without a man having ever retreated into its pure clarity, to remain there, in desire, held within its warmth.

I was swept up again in the bewilderment that had overpowered me when the corpse washers surrounded her and stripped off her clothes. Don't do this to her! Keep her covered by what covered her in life! The perplexing, awful sight of what they were doing upset and confused me so much that they had to drag me to a spot far enough away that I could see but only at a distance. Only so that I could observe my grandmother's body, there at the mercy of strangers' hands, she whom no hand had ever touched in her very long life. Some woman put her hand on my shoulder. "It's fine, Zuhour, you can be assured that it's all fine. We are covering her with sheets. We're protecting her modesty, shielding her in all these layers."

Later on, my sister, Sumayya, told me I was imagining things. She wasn't stripped of her clothes out in the open, it only happened behind sheets that curtained her, and no one else washed her body for the burial. Only us, and a few women who were helping us. Only us. Her grandchildren, who were not really her grandchildren. We who were not re-lated by blood. We washed her. "And you, Zuhour, you were screaming at people, so they took you away from it for a bit." But my sister is the one who was imagining things. I saw them! They were tearing off her masarr. She had kept her hair concealed but now it broke in white waves all over the place, everywhere, her hair that we washed and oiled once she no longer could do it, and then only occasionally. Ah, they have perfumed it now, Grandmother. Look, Maah— they have put aloe and camphor and musk on it. As you would never have dreamed we would do, in your final years on this treacherous deceitful earth. They perfumed your white waves of hair that no husband ever sought shade in.

Only the son and the son's children ever knew the shelter of that hair.

Her dead body looked nothing like her. It looked a lot like me.

When they laid out her corpse in our sitting room, I saw myself.

I crept away, as far as I could go. Away from her, away from me, away from my corpse laid out there for loved ones to mourn.

There were no loved ones other than us. Mansour, his wife, and his children, that's all. Those who came to gather around us only did so out of courtesy, or to please us.

The neighbor women came silently. They came to give us their solid assurances that we had done exactly what we ought to do, supporting the old woman in her weakness and illness, seeing her through her final years. They said to my mother, "You did all you could." They said to me and to my sister, "You didn't fall short." They said similar words to my father. "You did enough." As if she wasn't his mother, or the mother of his children, as if all her life she was only that old woman, crawling and crying out to us all, "Don't go." *Don't go!*

If our neighbor Shaykha had still been alive, she would have truly mourned. She loved my grandmother, and she probably felt in her bones, even after she had lost her senses, that my grandmother was the only person in the world who cared for her and knew how she felt in the years before her mind took its departure and began wandering down fantasy paths. Shaykha used to come by late in the morning, every day, to drink coffee with my grandmother. She didn't have a piece of mending in her hand, or a kumma ready to embroider, as the neighbor women always did. She came with empty hands, which were always ready to come to my grandmother's aid. Shaykha's hands picked through the fresh dates just off the trees, removed pits from dried dates, watered plants and trees, separated and peeled garlic cloves, removed the pith from the peel of dried lemons. Shaykha never talked about anything or anyone but her son, the angel who was kidnapped by a sly wicked jinni woman so she could take him into exile, to those foreign lands, the lands of the unbelievers. Those people who never washed the filth off their bodies and never asked for news of their own mothers.

And then we all got older. Me, my siblings, my grandmother; and our neighbor Shaykha. I would be studying in my room, my window open, and suddenly, there she was, my grandmother. I would see her springing up from the shade of the bitter orange tree to scurry toward the door. That's how I knew that our neighbor Shaykha had come out of her house again and over to ours without her trousers on, and that my grandmother would be taking her home and helping her get dressed again.

An hour later she would return to the shade of the na-rinjah tree, panting. I would guess, seeing her, that she must be seventy or so. And I would think, that whatever her exact age was, she was certainly the most determined person there could ever be. And, coming home from school, I would almost always come upon Shaykha, wandering through the lanes barefoot, her hand gripping a little coffee cup full of pounded rice. She would shriek at me. "Zuhour, Zuhour, have you seen Hamid? I've been looking all over for him since morning. He went out to play and he didn't come home. He didn't have his meal, the poor boy—I've pounded some rice for his lunch. If you see him, tell him to come home, his food is getting cold."

I would shake my head and move away quickly. My girlfriends from school would be laughing. Our neighbor Shaykha went on trudging through the narrow lanes, looking for her son who had emigrated forty years before, so that she could feed him the cupful of pounded rice. My grandmother was the only one who could get Shaykha to go home. She would put a plate over the rice, and show her where her sandals were, so that she wouldn't go out again in the hot sun without having them on.

We were not there to witness Shaykha's death. I don't know whether her corpse looked like her. It was the summer and we were in the Emirates. We'd been rewarded for our success in school with a trip to Hili Fun City. When we returned, happily weighed down with our plastic animals, brightly colored balls, and little diaries with pink hearts on the covers and gilt locks, we found our neighbor Shaykha's door locked. My grandmother told us that she had missed her for a whole day, so around the time for sunset prayers, she had gone over. She found Shaykha stretched out full-length, fully dressed, her shoes on her feet, surrounded by coffee cups holding ground rice that were giving off a fermented smell. She was dead.

Less than ten years later, we shut the door to my grandmother's room with a steel lock. She had died, gone silent, left the world as she lived in it, without a home, without a field, without a beloved to hold her close, without a brother to take care of her, and never having had children who came out of her own body.

The Gypsy Woman

B ut her corpse wasn't the first dead body I saw.

The ghagariyya. The gypsy woman—that's what we called her. Hers was the first dead body I saw. Sometimes the memory of it comes to me, like a whiff of rotting flowers.

The travelers' tents sat on the outskirts of the village. The gypsy woman arrived in our garden wearing a big silver nose ring from which dangled little crescent moons and stars. Her hand outstretched, she intoned, over and over, "Sahha bibiyya sahha bibiyya." Some dates for me, lady . . . I was very little when I heard her say that. I was rocking back and forth, standing on my grandmother's feet while she swung me back and forth. My mother muttered, "Filthy ghagariyya."

"Filthy—?" I repeated. My grandmother's elbow gave me a sharp poke and I didn't say anything more. A fading smell of old flowers, the distant memory, my grandmother's legs and feet that formed my little swing. My mother, after she took back the plate from which the woman had eaten the dates, scrubbing it seven times, the final time with dirt. Yes—my mother had counted, and I swung once for every number. Seven swings, and my grandmother's arms were tired, and my mother inside stopped scouring the plate.

The skin on the traveler woman's hand had been cracked, and there was a green tattoo on her chin. I was very little, and I don't remember whether it was my mother or grandmother who slapped me afterward when I said I wanted a necklace of colored beads like the one the gypsy woman wore.

Leaving our property, the woman plunged her bare feet into the pebbles. My sister, Sumayya, motioned at me, and the two of us followed her. We could stay far enough behind the woman, whichever alley she turned into, so that she would not see us. We avoided planting our feet where she had put hers down, because Sumayya said that *filthy* meant we couldn't touch anything she had touched, not even the dirt itself. We waited for her, lurking behind the doors of the houses she entered. She always came out either holding dates or with her clothes somehow looking dirtier than they had when she went in. She was a very long time in the house of Hamid the widower. So long that we almost forgot all about her, as we went about chasing other children up and down the lane. Finally, she emerged, pulling her headscarf tighter around her face, as she gazed down at a shiny coin in her hand. The ringing sound that the stars and crescent moons made as they collided against one another attracted me, and her beads looked as though they were lit from within by tiny lights. But I was afraid to tell Sumayya that I wanted a string of beads just like that. Sumayya might hit me, too. The boys called out to us. Sumayya dived into the band of boys who were from our immediate neighborhood. She pushed up her sleeves and ordered me to go home. That's because Ulyan and Fattoum were on the other side and they would beat me. Sumayya said she wouldn't be able to fend them off, because she already had to face up against some types who were more menacing than Ulyan and Fattoum. So I went home.

It was days later—or maybe it was hours later, I don't remember, since when one is a child, time does not really exist. It was nearly sunset, I do remember that very clearly. And it wasn't like the vanishing smell of dead flowers . . . it was a clear, pure sunset of beautiful tones, like colored beads. It was a sunset in which the men were gathered for prayer at the mosque, while the women, at home, were bent over their preparations for dinner. And the children discovered the dead body.

The clear, beautiful sunset and the dead body. My memory of that day. The gypsy woman with the green tattoo and the big silver nose ring, lying there, eyes fixed and blood pouring from her chest. The children squatted down, stirring the blood into the dirt, making little balls and wads, but I didn't move. I saw the colored beads from her necklace had rolled loose, the string broken. The beads sat near the woman's neck and I didn't dare to go over and pick them up. I don't know how long it was before any grown-ups came along that little back way or when they chased away the children. Did they give them a severe scolding for making balls out of dirt and blood? Did they get angry because the children had been so engrossed in their games that they didn't bother to tell the adults right away? I don't know, I don't remember. Now, memory becomes a vanishing fragrance, this memory is gone, and this is where the pure, calm sunset fades into nothing.

Love Sets Conditions

Every time I was with Kuhl, she told me—over and over, she told me—that she was going to confess everything to her family, and then make her marriage permanent, and live it, out in the open. But despite these decisions, months passed without her taking a single step to implement them. She was terrified at the prospect of a confrontation with her family.

One early afternoon in late autumn, we were watching the leaves fall, like mute witnesses to a paradise being lost before our eyes. Suroor was sitting between us, her slight, delicate frame rigidly straight, while Kuhl and I were leaning back in our seats. But when our eyes met, I had to acknowledge how inadequate people's little strategems tend to be. All those ties and constraints that people really believe they have undone on their way through life, with all the steep and difficult leaps that life holds. What I saw was despair. I saw Kuhl's thin paper kite colliding with one lamppost after another as it climbed skyward, and then tore to shreds.

"If only my family's love wasn't *on condition*." Her voice was low, more like a quiet sob than a set of words.

"Their love for us doesn't set any conditions," Suroor said.

Kuhl didn't speak again right away. But then: "If only their love weren't conditional on my following a path determined by their choices."

Suroor was uncomfortable with the direction this conversation was taking. Her face darkened and abruptly she suggested that we go to get coffee at the corner kiosk, a tiny place barely big enough for the vendor and his barista equipment. We cupped our hands around the warm, delicious, welcoming brew. It was a pleasant distraction for Kuhl, even if it was only a fleeting one.

What I was seeing now was a kite that Sumayya and I had made for Sufyan, a little boy at the time. We spent hours with my grandmother, making a frame out of firm reed stems that she had gathered from the fields of our village. I could see the long, shiny ribbons dangling from the kite, glistening in the cold autumn sun. Their shine seemed reflected in Kuhl's eyes. In a different way, the ribbons seemed to twist, glinting, around Suroor's slim fingers and onto the cup of coffee. Did my grandmother's love set conditions? Her love just seemed there, simple, like the air that meant I could breathe, without thinking about it; given freely and generously, bestowed as the sun gives its light, freely enough to allow me to see my way ahead. Her love had to be deserved, it was true; but it left no obligation. My grandmother never made me feel—or made my father or brother or sister feel—that we were in debt to her. We deserved her as we deserved to be alive, and breathing, and turning our faces to the sun.

The White Room

I was sitting in a deep, roomy leather armchair and he sat facing me. Not facing me exactly. He was at an angle to me, turned a bit toward one corner of the room, and surely that was deliberate. On the table before me was a box of tissues in case this was going to involve any tears, and a little wooden clock in case I had too much to say. There was a large window in this room, and rain was running down the expanse of it. The walls were white. He hardly said a word. It was me who was talking—and talking and talking. After an hour, his eyes flitted to the clock in front of me. I understood, and I got to my feet immediately, being sure to thank him.

My friend Christine had advised me to go to see him, when I told her I was feeling sad. In her culture, she said, there was a solution to every problem, even sadness. And so that's what I did: I sought a solution to this problem of mine, although not very seriously. I wrote down the date and time of the appointment and I met with him in this room. I met with him several times, in fact. Every time I was in that room, rain was running down that enormous window.

I didn't talk to him about my grandmother. I didn't say anything about the *Don't go*s that, late at night, echoed from one side of my skull to the other, reminding me that I had gone. I didn't tell him about not knowing why her thumbnail was disfigured and black. I didn't ask him about the oh-so-thin threads that are tied to the tails of life's paper kites. Or the thick rope—thick perhaps, but still invisible—that separates what one understands from the empathy one feels for people.

What did we talk about, in the white room, seeking a treatment for sadness? Was it perhaps something about my father, or my mother? About Imran and Kuhl? My studies? The trap of language? I don't remember now. Anyway, at the time, was I even aware of such a thing as the trap of language? I don't recall. Did I really say something to him about feeling disabled because of language? I don't think so. If I had said anything like that, he would not have noticed it anyway. He would not have detected this trap. He didn't see me as disabled, bound to a wheelchair that was language's incapacity to fully express me. No, no. We didn't have any discussions about traps of any kind. He wanted to know, plain and simple, the reasons for my sadness. Like him, I wanted to know those, too.

Our appointments were scheduled for Fridays every week. I didn't know when or how I was supposed to assume that these Friday meetings would now draw to a close. But I discontinued them of my own accord after three or four sessions. I told myself that in the end, sadness is not an illness. Or perhaps I found it all rather futile—the way he drilled into me, searching for the reasons behind my sadness. In the women's toilets you always saw notices plastered around urging you to dial a free number to get advice. "If you've no one to talk to, we listen." Sometimes they explained, in bullet points, the symptoms of depression. Other notices were specifically about advice on sex and unwanted pregnancies. The word *depression* terrified me. My mother was never completely cured of it, and I was mortally afraid of turning out to be like my mother. Many times, Christine had reminded me of Oscar Wilde's words: "All women become like their mothers. That is their tragedy." The first words I said to the counselor in the white room with the rain rolling down the windowpane were: "I am not depressed."

I was in the hunter's trap. I believed that one day, some little rodent would chew a hole in the wire that surrounded me on all sides, and would free me. Any rodent, any fate, but as I waited for it to bite, the wire settled itself around me more firmly. Where was the bite that would be my salvation? What I didn't realize was that I was the rodent. By the time I did understand that, all my verminous teeth had fallen out.

The Wood Gatherer and the Lion

I woke up suddenly in the middle of the night. I was sleeping on my side, and for whatever reason, the idea of my own death was there in my head. What really overwhelmed me, what I couldn't shake, was a powerful sense of nonexistence. I was nothing, I thought. We are only tiny specks in this universe, crumbs that will return to nothing, as they were before, while the cosmos will just keep on expanding for millions more years. But I felt deeply accepting of this concept, the idea of my own death; in fact, I felt it so strongly that I almost smiled at the intensity of it—this openness to my own disappearance, or my nonbeing. I didn't feel any anxiety about it, nor even much curiosity. Nothing more than musing about how it would happen and perhaps what the timing would be; those questions about my own mortality did come to me, but even those questions soon were gone. I felt completely at ease, confident, composed, tranquil. Breathing deeply. As if I had come to terms with something. I went back to sleep.

As my grandmother was combing my hair and oiling

it with coconut oil in the shade of the bitter orange tree, I asked her, "Why did your father throw you out when you were little?"

She finished plaiting my hair into two braids and turned me around to face her. "Zuhour, dear," she said, "when the Lord takes something away from His servant, the Lord makes up for it with something else."

"But if my father threw me out," I said, "nothing could make up for it."

She rubbed my head and said reassuringly, "Mansour? No, it's not something he would ever do."

I went to sleep on her lap, burrowed into her crossed legs. As I was falling asleep, she was telling me a story. "There was a wood gatherer whose wife tormented him. But he was a patient man, and he just kept going into the scrubland to gather his wood. Every time he had gathered just enough to carry back, a lion would appear, offering his back. The man put his load of wood on the lion's bent back, and the lion carried it for him, all the way home.

"One day, the wood gatherer's wife died. Now he had relief from her perpetual scolding. But after her death, when he went out to gather more wood, the lion did not appear. The man looked for him, looked and looked, but there was no lion in sight. Instead, he saw an angel from heaven appear before him. The angel said, 'We gave you the lion as compensation, because you were so patient about your wife's unceasing persecution, but now she has died and so the lion is gone.'"

When my grandmother died, the bitter orange tree died, too. Day after day, it withered a little more until it was completely dried out. In vain we watered it, each taking our turn, and my father replaced the dirt just beneath and around it with fresh soil. He bought fertilizer, and the Bengali who worked for us enlisted the help of his friends who worked on farms. They poured all their experience into the bitter orange tree, but it didn't respond to anyone's efforts. The narinjah had made up its mind, and before the soil over my grandmother's burial place was dry, it had stopped sucking in water and air. It began to give off a smell of rot. The odor of goodbye.

Why did the story happen in reverse? Why, when my grandmother died, did the lion vanish even though she was my good sweet grandma? Did my grandmother know that the bitter orange tree she had planted with her own hands was the lion who would go away as soon as she had departed? But this story happened the wrong way around. The losses piled up, and there was nothing there to compensate for them. No compensation, Grandmother. Maah.

The Dynamo

It was during one of those Friday meetings in the white room with the rain smattering down the window. Perhaps it was the second or third Friday? All I remember is that it was the same Friday on which Kuhl introduced me, after my session, to Imran. To her husband.

On that particular Friday, I told the counselor about my sister, Sumayya. I told him the nickname she had in our family: the Dynamo. From the moment she had sprung out of my mother's body, she had never stopped moving. When we were little, if she wasn't jumping rope or chasing after cats, or hunting lizards or setting traps for birds, or scurrying up the little hill behind the house, or trying to scale the walls or climbing the bitter orange tree or shimmying up the young date palms, she would be talking rapid-fire and laughing loud enough that everyone around could hear.

Sumayya was older than I was. When she began middle school, my father relented and agreed she was old enough to have a Sony cassette deck with big speakers. When we went to the Emirates that summer, she spent all the money she had saved on cassettes by Samira Saʻid and Amr Diab.

The counselor raised his blond eyebrows.

"No, you wouldn't know them," I said. "It's okay. They're Arab singers." Sumayya was obsessed with them, listening to them day and night and dancing to them in her little room.

He responded in that voice, so well trained to sound smoothly understanding and sympathetic. "And what was your relationship like?"

My laugh must have sounded abrupt. "Sumayya and me? Let me explain something to you. First came Sumayya, and then a miscarriage, and then me. And then two more miscarriages, and Sufyan, and another miscarriage. There's three years between Sumayya and me, and six or seven between me and Sufyan. Six years you can't dismiss. But Sumayya and I, we didn't pay much attention to the three years between us. We fought sometimes, but we were always laughing. I went to primary school in the afternoons, while she went to middle school in the mornings. When I came home around sunset, she would be waiting for me on the bench in front of the house. We told each other everything that had happened at school that day. I couldn't keep up with her when it came to jumping and climbing and sliding, nor in dancing later on, but I was just as good as she was when it came to making up funny names for the teachers. The science teacher, who always wore a green dress, was Kermit the Frog from *Sesame Street*. The math teacher, who was massive, we called the Mandus, because she was like one of our mother's big wooden chests. The skinny art teacher was Tweety Bird. We used to replace these names with others, now and then."

He interrupted me for the first time. "You're talking about her in the past tense. What happened?"

I smiled weakly. "She stopped moving. The Dynamo came to an end."

Actually I did not say to him that Sumayya "came to an end" or that she "stopped moving." That's what I meant, but the language trap disabled me. Trying to use this other language, I could not say what I truly wanted to say. I probably said something like "She lost energy" or "She went into a decline." But what I heard inside myself was "she stopped moving." Sumayya the Dynamo had become still and silent.

I wanted to run through the rain, to catch up with Kuhl and Imran in the little café, the Three Monkeys, that would eventually become our favorite. I wanted to tell them that Sumayya the Dynamo had come to an end, and that my grandmother had died, and that she never owned a plot of land, not even a single tree.

A Day Trip

When Sumayya's husband announced that tomorrow they would make a day trip to the ancient mountainside village and gardens of Misfat al-Abriyin, he had not asked her beforehand what she thought of the idea, or even told her in advance that they were going. The only reason he was telling her now was so that she would know to get herself ready.

They had been married only a few weeks when Sumayya realized that there was never going to be any real conversation between the two of them. Her husband was to be the center around which everything had to pivot. Anything on the margins of his world he was unable to see or hear or think about. Anything outside of his own self he considered utterly peripheral, a distant site, remote from the focus of his concerns. Very soon indeed after the wedding, Sumayya saw clearly that she was one of those distant sites.

The next morning, Sumayya made sandwiches and filled a thermos with milky tea. She put on a long blue tunic over jeans. Before she could wrap her sheela around her head, her husband clapped his hands on either side of her face and squeezed it hard between his palms. Sumayya did not make a sound. He laughed. "My strong little sweetie," he said. "My pretty doll." She waited until he removed his hands, and then she silently resumed getting dressed. She got into the car and waited for him.

It was a fresh, brisk morning toward the end of February. Her husband was in a good mood. On the way, he hummed a few of Salim al-Suri's old tunes, and he reminisced about his time as a student in Australia. Chuckling, he described the bodies of the girls who used to fight for the privilege of devoting themselves to him.

Even as the morning advanced, the freshness remained in the air. Sumayya closed her eyes, hearing what she thought was the sweet, melodic chirping of birds. He gripped her shoulder and gave it a hard shake. Her eyelids flew open. "Don't go off to sleep and leave me all alone," he barked. "I didn't get married and lose my freedom just for the sake of a dumb statuette who has nothing to say."

The birdsong disappeared. Sumayya stared at her fingernails, noticing how short they were, and how perfectly rounded.

He stopped the car. He selected a tree and stood leaning against it, waiting for Sumayya to spread out the mat and pour the tea. He sat down across from her and began to eat.

The leaves on the tree above them were motionless; suddenly, the heaviness of noon had fallen. The light was dazzling. Somewhere, a ewe bleated, and then a flock of sheep followed. There came into view a shepherd girl, her distinctive whistle signaling her sheep, who massed together obediently.

Sumayya smiled at the shepherd girl, but the girl didn't seem to see her. Sumayya's husband already understood that if his wife smiled, it must be because of something outside of his control, something apart, a place distant from the center of his self. A silly little shepherd girl could make her smile! He put down his sandwich and began gulping his tea.

Now the shepherd girl noticed them. She was wearing a well-worn blue dishdasha and slippers that were coming apart. But her teeth, as she smiled at Sumayya, were dazzlingly white. Sumayya waved to her. Sumayya's husband hurled his glass of tea at the tree trunk.

Sumayya shrank back. The veins flared on his temples as he lurched toward her. "Have you forgotten that I like my tea strong? This tea tastes of nothing. *Strong*. Don't you understand anything at all?"

They had gone to Thailand on their honeymoon. When papaya fruits dropped onto the hotel room's glass balcony with a loud thud, the veins in his temples had throbbed visibly. But he hadn't raised his voice. Sumayya—brand-new bride Sumayya—was bewildered by it. She tried to talk to him about it, to ask what the problem was. He slammed his fist into her mouth.

Before they were even back from Thailand, he had shattered a vase, two plates, a cup, and the little finger of her right hand.

Now he inched toward her, silently. Still seated, she kept pushing herself back, until she felt her spine bumping the tree trunk. Fragments of glass cut her hands. She knew by now that when he was breaking things and the blue veins were bulging along his face, any word she said would cause the next breakage. That it had happened before did not lessen the terror she felt. All she could hope, in this silent tableau, was that he would start to shout or scream, because she thought that was the only thing that might possibly unfreeze her legs. If he screamed, she might be able to run. To flee. But he didn't raise his voice. Ever.

His eyes were red and his breaths slapped her face. Sumayya, trembling, pressed herself back, harder and harder, against the tree trunk. A sudden gust of wind brought with it the smell of sheep dung. She could hear a crow caw in the distance. The wind grew strong enough to dislodge some pebbles at the edges of the mat. By the time her husband finally stepped back, Sumayya had wet her clothes through.

He stared at the spot on her trousers. He didn't seem to know what it meant. Looking puzzled—or astonished—he brought her tissues from the car. He tried to dry the spot, and then to scrub her hands free of the effects of the glass shards and the blood. He put his arms around her, and whispered, "Don't be afraid, my doll. I am your husband. I'm your lover. There's no reason to be afraid."

Bliss

I could see my grandmother coming down the stairs, leaning on her cane. The sight brought a rush of affection and concern; I was afraid that she might slip and fall, and I hurried to help her. She put her weight on me and mumbled a few words. Something like "waiting for you."

"I haven't seen you for a long time," I said. "I've missed you."

"I see you," she said.

"I haven't seen you for a long time," I repeated. "I've missed you." She was silent. When we had reached the bottom of the stairs, she said, "I'm not hearing you." So I spoke more loudly. But she only shook her head, to tell me she could not hear me. I had the sensation that suddenly she had gotten much older. "Are we nearly there yet? Much farther to go?" she asked.

"A little more," I said. "But we can rest for a few minutes, if you like." I sat down. I sat her in my lap. I couldn't help looking at her hair. A thick layer of dirt had dried on it, making it stiff. It shocked me that things had gone this far. I started trying to scrape the dried mud from her hair, until it was falling onto my hands. I burst out crying. She seemed to sense what I was going through. Tears ran down her face.

"What is it?" she asked.

"Nothing," I answered.

I had seen this dream before.

I had this dream the night my sister, Sumayya—my sister the bride—came back to our house. But that time, when my grandmother asked me, in the dream, "What is it?" all I could say was "Our world has collapsed. Our world, which you kept balanced on your head, like the clay jahla."

Sumayya had returned from her Thailand honeymoon. She came from her honeymoon directly to our house, suitcase and all.

"I'm not going back to him," she said to my father and mother.

"What're you complaining about?" my father asked. "What's wrong with him?"

"He frightens me."

She stayed with us for several days, crying the entire time. Her nerves were a mess. The neighbor women whispered things to one another, and wherever she went, intrusive questions followed her. His family came to negotiate.

Sumayya didn't show them her little finger, broken. She bowed her head and lived with the struggle that was tearing at her mind.

He came. He kissed her feet in the presence of my parents, who were bewildered by it all and didn't know what to think. He told them that she was in his possession, and he was in hers, and he would not be able to live for even one moment without his wife, his beloved.

For the second time, Sumayya left our house, dragging her suitcase behind her.

A month later, she was back. She couldn't stop trembling. He came to the house to beg her to return. He threatened that he would harm himself. He lined up the gifts, and he scattered flowers all the way from our home's front entrance to the doorway of her room. And so she did go back with him. And once again, he forced her to circle around him as stars orbit the center of their galaxy. In less than a year, no one was using her old name, Sumayya the Dynamo. She was just Sumayya now.

When she had still been Sumayya the Dynamo, she danced in joyous celebration of her handsome fiancé, and she sat next to him on the fancy, ornate wedding couch. Her longed-for state of bliss was so close, she thought, that she could almost touch it.

But those brief days of her engagement ended, and she was still waiting for this impending bliss. She could almost see it there, envision what it would be like. She almost felt it was so close she could tap it on the shoulder, and then maybe it would turn around and attend to her needs. But waiting for this bliss of hers was like waiting for that one drop of liquid, sliding along the rim of a cup, waiting for it to roll down the side—and this cup was not even hers.

Her tongue was out, waiting, and she could see the drop slipping along the edge of the cup. She could all but taste the pleasant tang of it. But the drop rolled slowly. The drop was heavy. The sides of the cup drank it in before she could. When it reached the bottom and her waiting tongue, it had already dissolved. It had become part of the cup itself.

Sumayya said to herself, "Maybe the drop of bliss will slide into me along with the wedding, or as soon as the wedding takes place and is over." And the wedding did take place.

More than a year later, on their outing to Misfat al-Abriyin, she was plagued by obscure sensations that her husband was going to slip while walking along the stones edging the pool. That little wet yellow leaf that had fallen from the mango tree—she could see it there—would make him slip. The thought froze her. In her dreams, eternally, she would go on seeing those two paces that separated her from him. She would see that as he walked, his shoulders were rigid and high, as always; hers were bowed, as always. She would see that his leather sandals were wet and her athletic shoes were dry. In her dreams, they would continue walking along the rim of the pool. The two-step distance between them would remain two steps, no more and no less. But this was a scene held hostage to dreams; and eventually, dreams fade and vanish.

In real life, the interval between those two paces was a single instant, one moment in time, after which she did not take another step. Any step. She was frozen in place there, and frozen in place forever.

A Leaf Falling from the Mango Tree

Sumayya stayed next to the tree until her clothes had dried. She wanted to go home so that she could take a bath. But he insisted that they would go on. There was no trace of any smell on her, he asserted, now that the noonday sun had dried her clothes.

She didn't attempt to argue. He rolled up the mat. She picked up the one unbroken glass and the thermos. They left the uneaten sandwiches for the animals and drove away.

The entire way, Sumayya stared straight ahead. The late-afternoon sky was beautiful and clear, and her husband was silent. When they reached the lovely village of Birkat al-Mouz, at the foot of the Jabal Akhdar, she saw some boys kicking around a rubber ball. In the late-afternoon sun, endless points of winking light reverberated off every kick. Her husband stopped to buy two cups of tea. Slowly, Sumayya read the sign outside the shop. LAHZAT SHAY. A Moment for Tea. She closed her eyes and saw the word *Moment* magnified. She opened her eyes and continued reading, slowly; it seemed to take some effort. *We have: masala chai, rosehip tea, saffron tea, cinnamon tea, zaatar tea* . . . Her husband handed her the hot tea. Putting her hands around the paper cup, she felt a sharp sting from the cuts on her palms.

Now the car was climbing the mountain road to Misfat al-Abriyin. A thin white thread of cloud wound and twisted through the sky. Sumayya saw a paper kite that had escaped its owner, floating on its own, high above them. She recognized it, in fact. She and Zuhour had made this kite for Sufyan when he was little. They made it out of colored paper and reeds, and they decorated it with shiny stripes. Their grandmother had fetched from the fields the reeds that made its spine, and her mother bought the streamers that they attached to it.

By the time they reached the village, the thread of cloud was even thinner and Sumayya could no longer see the kite. She got out of the car and walked with her husband. The horizon glowed red. The pebbles jumped from beneath their feet. Her steps were heavy. She was trying to avoid being close to anyone, worried that they would be able to make out her smell. And she was trying to lag behind so that he would not be beside her.

The stone stairs and the little stone bridges seemed like they would go on forever. Her steps grew slower. The sun was setting. She felt utterly exhausted and could barely walk, but she didn't say anything.

They were getting closer to the fields. She could smell fruit left to rot at the bases of the trees. The sun dropped below the horizon and she heard the call to prayer. She had kept her eyes on her husband's feet the entire way, always a few steps ahead of hers. He was wearing backless sandals, and the soles of his feet were very pale. She stopped, suddenly. She saw the paper kite, its ribbons still sparkly, her grandmother's reeds as strong and firm as ever. Sumayya stretched out her hand, but the kite swooped away.

The half-darkness was spreading softly through the palm trees. She and her husband descended the stone steps that led down to the orchards. A small, deep pool lay there, its brimming waters set to pour into the main canals and then to water the trees. She saw his feet stop moving, and so hers stopped as well. She saw his feet turning, to follow the raised stone rim around the small pool.

Before Sumayya could follow her husband, she heard the splashing made by the men performing their ablutions in the shallow ford nearby. Her eyes traced the last remnants of light playing on the men's white dishdashas as they mounted the steep stone steps to the tiny mosque above the pool, glowing faintly in the light of one solitary lamp.

Her feet were dragging by now. But she mounted the wall around the pool, following her husband's feet. He walked slowly; she stayed slightly behind him. She was wearing her athletic shoes; he was in leather sandals. Her shoes were dry; his were slightly wet by now. All she could see was the white glimmer of the backs of his feet, as she followed them. That was the moment in which she caught sight of the mango leaf, and then suddenly, he slipped.

Sumayya stood at the edge of the pool. Her husband was not a swimmer, and he had fallen into the dark, deep pool. His head bobbed below the surface as he fought the water, trying to save himself and calling out to her. With the sharp smell of urine rising from her clothes in her nostrils, Sumayya did not move. She could tell that he was struggling to breathe as he attempted to reach the edge. Her eyes stayed on him as she heard the voices of the men at their prayers, faint and far away. Her tongue felt heavy. The sign A MO-MENT FOR TEA blinked on and off in her head, the word *Moment* growing larger and larger with every blink.

Her husband was drowning, and she stood there unable to move. The men finished the cycle of sunset prayers. They came out of the mosque and broke into scattered conversations, the affectionate tones of friends, as they descended the steps.

It was growing darker. Her husband was silent and still now.

A man yelled, "Someone's drowned!"

They pulled him from the water, his body swollen, and

tried to save him, but he was already dead. When the men finally noticed Sumayya, rigid and still, she was standing in the same precise spot. "How long have you been here?" one of them called out. He raised his voice. "You didn't shout? We would have heard you if you had."

"To God is all power and might," exclaimed another. "The woman is in shock, take her inside." Some women appeared and took her into someone's house. They rolled out a mattress and began asking her questions. "The poor man— was he your husband?" Sumayya didn't say a word.

"If it was her husband, she's got to start her idda now," someone said. An elderly woman pressed her hand against Sumayya's head. "Say it with me, my dear. Allahumma fi niyyati w'itiqadi inni u'taddu ala zawji al-haalik arbaatushur w-ashrata iyyam taa'atan lillah wa-li-rasulih. I swear my intention and belief to remain chaste to my late husband for four months and ten days in obedience to God and His Messenger." Sumayya's eyes were wide open; her mouth remained shut. The women removed her thin gold bangles and her wedding ring. "Find her family," one of the women said. "Do what needs to be done. Subhaana Allah . . . I'm smelling urine."

Nostalgia

Johannes Hofer was a medical student. Like Imran.

Imran suffered his longings in silence. More than three hundred years before Imran enrolled in medical school, Johannes Hofer coined the term *nostalgia*. He joined the word *nóstos*, "return," with *algia*, meaning "pain." Hofer inserted this new word into the title of his dissertation on the malady experienced by Swiss soldiers far from their mountain homes. Imran suppressed the sickness in his heart.

A Ukrainian student who worked as a waitress in the Three Monkeys Café brought our coffee. I always imagined the monkeys on the big posters behind us grinning every time one of us took delight in the rich froth of this café's coffee. Imran first stirred sugar into Kuhl's cup and then into his own. Something about the way he did it forced me to see a residue of sickness in his heart, almost invisible, like grains of sugar melting into coffee. Picture the distant fields in isolated villages that didn't have names.

The mother's tarha, torn and rubbed gritty from the soil beneath the crops. Her silver earrings—all the wealth she had. The gray sunset over the rusty dull metal of the train that carried the wheat and cotton away from the village. The high-pitched, piercing little cackles of his baby sister as her body shook, laced to the donkey's back so that she wouldn't slip off.

Nostalgia floated to the surface of his eyes momentarily, and then I saw it melt into the first sip of coffee.

He was very, *very* charming.

Kuhl said she had decided that he must be descended from the line of Mughal princes who had ruled the Indian subcontinent. He looked exactly like the portraits that had been done of Jahangir, one of the greatest bon vivants among the Mughals of the seventeenth century. I didn't comment. As far as I was concerned, Imran didn't look like anyone else, and no one looked like him. Imran was one of a kind.

Kuhl always wore embroidered tunics with high collars and long sleeves, over jeans. She picked out hijabs that corresponded to the colors of her kurtas and the flats she always wore. Imran wore striped shirts and different-colored trousers, along with matching scarves. He was very careful with his appearance, so scrupulous that it seemed to me he must go through agonies before every outing with her, since he clearly wanted to be absolutely certain that every detail was appropriate and harmonious. There was no doubt in my mind that he was working some part-time job on the side, along with his studies, at the very least in order to cover what must be a formidable clothing budget.

"Let's have something sweet," Kuhl said brightly. They left the choice to me. I chose apple tart with vanilla ice cream. Kuhl laughed, because apple tart reminded her of Grandma Elvira Duck in the Donald Duck cartoons. Imran looked at the floor, as he did every time Kuhl spoke about something from her childhood. That told me he'd had nothing like it in his own early days.

Imran never watched any cartoons as a child. He didn't know what a magazine was until, as a secondary school student, he went on a school trip to Lahore. Not long after that, he was awarded the scholarship to come here. It wasn't Imran who told me this but Kuhl. She told me all about his childhood long before I ever met him. He never talked very much, anyway. Now he carefully cut the apple tart into portions. I couldn't help noticing how slim and long his fingers were.

The café was empty except for us, which was unusual. The Ukrainian waitress was humming a tune from home as she studied her textbook. When Imran got up to pay the bill, she said a few words to him about her upcoming exams. His response was even briefer. Did he wish to appear uninterested in people, or was it just that he didn't find it easy to communicate?

Whatever the case, he certainly was captivating.

The Color Blue

Sumayya stares at her hands and wrists. They are bare now. No gold bangles, no diamond wedding ring.

Her nails are long, shaped into careful half-circles, and she can see the traces of old wounds on her palms from the shards of a shattered glass tumbler. Staring into her hands, Sumayya sees the intense late-morning light reflected. A dazzlingly bright late morning, for two suns appear to her, giving off light. Sumayya can see a heavy rope stretched between the two suns. At one end dangles a tunic of hers, long and blue, and at the other end, farther away, hangs a worn blue dishdasha belonging to a shepherd girl.

Sumayya keeps looking at her hands. It is her hands that have created this heavy late-morning scene, just before noon. Sumayya sees herself hanging by her hands on the heavy rope, swinging between the two suns. Now her body touches her tunic, and now it touches the shepherd girl's dishdasha. The wounds on her palms open. Thin threads of blood run from them, and her flesh tears. Sumayya cannot stop looking at her hands. She cannot open her mouth to moan in pain.

Bonds of Sympathy

A sympathetic bond and a mutual fondness grew between my grandmother and Athurayyaa. The deeper Bint Aamir's hands plunged into the household—into the soil, planting the family's trees; into the bread dough, kneading it; into the oven, to bake the bread; onto little Mansour's body, scrubbing it with a loofah and soap—the higher Athurayyaa rose above the soil, above the earth, circling in the air of our home until she was part of the air we breathed. She rose into the atmosphere with her prayer rug, like a ghost. Bint Aamir's feet were submerged in the soil that was the ground of our lives. She built the walls that made this household exist and thrive, mud brick by mud brick. Athurayyaa ascended higher and higher, building a world of purely spiritual bricks. Athurayyaa inscribed amulets to keep fever away from children. She mixed saffron into a bit of water and painted Qur'an verses onto the interiors of shallow white cups. Once the lettering had dried, women in labor added water and drank the mixture to lessen their pain. People came to her seeking other cures and she responded, without charge and without a word. Her hopes were heavenward, and her desires did not include the recompenses of this world.

Bint Aamir had to walk through the soil of this world. To escape the sting of the late-morning sun, she would bind palm fronds to the bottom of her feet with thongs made of palm fiber. She balanced the clay jahla on her head and drew water from the falaj, Mansour following her every step. He was old enough now that he took pleasure in flaunting the myriad tiny round mirrors along the hems and front edges of his little broadcloth robes. These outer garments, shot through with gold threads, were ordered especially for him from India. He tried to provoke Bint Aamir by holding the mirrors up to the sun so the rays would bounce off them and straight into her one good eye. But she did not react; on her head, the jahla sat as steady as ever. When he tired of trying unsuccessfully to goad her, he gave up and ran ahead of her, toward the house, where his mother Athurayyaa had washed herself in preparation for midday prayers, pushing her soft feet into her wooden Zanzibari clogs. She walked across the courtyard to her prayer niche and began saying supererogatory prayers to the movement of her beads as she waited for the call to prayer. By now, his father, Salman, would have closed the door to his shop, ready for his midday nap, leaving Mansour to snitch sugar cubes from the tin that had on its lid a scene of a summer day in England, women in frocks and parasols walking among the trees. Mansour always imagined himself in that scene, racing ahead of his friends.

By now, Mansour was approaching the age of twelve, when his father would shave off his braids. The winds of fortune were finally blowing in Salman's direction. He earned hundreds of silver thalers in a windfall deal that no one could have foreseen. Athurayyaa opened the doors of the household to the needy. Pots were hung over the fire. Women from much poorer families flocked to the household of Salman, to measure out wheat flour, which they kneaded into loaves and baked on the premises. They cleaned rice and boiled it, staying there through the midday hours. In the late afternoon, they carried the bread and the rice and their pots of yogurt to their own homes.

One evening, one of the neighbor women suggested to Athurayyaa and Bint Aamir that they ought to order silver bolts for their carved wood chests, and have gold latticework made for their rosewater vials. A wealthy woman of the village had been famous for having such things once. Silently, Athurayyaa went back to her prayer rug. Bint Aamir looked this neighbor and her advice in the eye and said, "Go home and give your advice to somebody else. No envy here of the rich lady, and we certainly aren't going to do what she did. The envious imitate others only because they've got nothing better to do."

The woman went home and never came back. Bint Aamir did fear the envy of others, and she always took precautions against its searing flame. But when envy did do its evil work, it came as a terrible blow, which no one could have predicted, and it flattened her without any warning, at least for a time. For it was only a couple of months after this encounter with the silver-bolt woman that the twins, Rayyaa and Raayah, landed in Salman's home as his guests. Their arrival did not appear to change anything in Bint Aamir's life in this household, nor did it temper the well-deserved recognition she got for being such a devoted mother to Mansour. But strange, foreign doors had been opened now, and obscure fears invaded her already anxious heart.

When Rayyaa and Raayah's father had found himself caught in the snare of an ill-fated marriage, he worked several ruses to try to get out of it. A series of minor attempts at escape failed, but then he was given a chance to travel far away. He embarked for the Congo leaving two little girls in his wife's care as well as the grove of date palms, which shriveled and died in the drought that fell two years after he left.

He thought he had rid himself, as much as he could, of those burdens of dependency that had so worn him down. He believed he could congratulate himself on having managed to elude all but the inevitable setbacks. Moreover, he had developed a passion for going deep into the Congo Basin rain forests on leopard-hunting expeditions—a venture that kept him free of the irritations that invariably arise in human interactions. But just when he had become most impervious to those annoying responsibilities of his past, or so he thought, a letter in the mail took him by surprise. His wife had died. She had died—just as she had lived—without knowing any happiness, any desires, any ambitions. His twin daughters were orphans now and completely alone. The date palms had long since died, too, and the land had been sold.

He had to wake from his fairy-tale escapades, landing in the dirt of the real world and sensing the noose of blood ties around his neck. His only recourse was to write to a relative in Oman, Hilal, a man renowned for his piety. He asked Hilal to fetch his daughters, and Hilal took on the burden of his relative's plight. He booked passage and loaded the two girls—not even ten years old at the time, they were impossible to tell apart, one as emaciated as the other—on a ship from the port of Sur bound for Zanzibar. Onboard, a sudden blood clot ended Hilal's life. As his body was lowered into the sea, the two little girls began to wail. They clasped each other's hands and did not let go until the ship had anchored off the coast of Zanzibar and disgorged its passengers.

When the twins arrived onshore, they found that Hilal's corpse had washed onto the land before they had. People wept for the pious man whose body had not been touched by the sea's sharks nor by the vultures of the sky. They buried him among the graves of sainted men, and the girls went with their father, who had come to meet them in Zanzibar, to the Congo. They grew up there in near-total isolation from other people. Their father periodically forgot they existed, so they taught themselves how to grow cassava and bananas, keeping their stomachs full and selling the surplus. On the fringes of the rain forest, their bodies grew, and they wrapped them in kanga cloth. The sisters planted and harvested, and went hunting with their father. Sometimes he did remember to bring them food. Always, he remembered to force them to speak Arabic. But he forgot completely to see about getting them married. When he died, they knew very well that they were alone in the world.

After a long period of indecision, Rayyaa and Raayah decided to go back to Oman. They could not remember anything about their life there, or their family. The sisters tried hard to recall the details of the existence they had had with their long-departed mother, and they tried to remember some good moments. But the only times they could remember their mother's eyes lighting up with enthusiasm, the only glint of interest she ever showed in anything in this world, were those moments when she heard news of someone's death, or when she recalled—with the kind of detail that most minds repel—how she had learned of these death notices. But Rayyaa and Raayah came back anyway. They learned that Salman was their nearest living relative. Or, perhaps, that he was their most generous relative. And so they landed in the hospitality of his home.

When Rayyaa and Raayah alighted as guests in the household of Salman, they came with wooden clogs and small bundles of clothing—very few clothes, but all clean, and all perfumed with incense. They also had with them a small wooden chest that held a few silver pieces, and another bundle, tied up with care. This one they opened to reveal the marvel of marvels, which was to remain the talk of the village for weeks to come: a real, whole leopard skin.

They came prepared to stay in this home of Salman their generous relative. What they found when they arrived was a man preoccupied with his trade, a woman engrossed in her prayers, and a young teen who played in the alleyways. They found no one who might engage with them face-to-face, no one who would leave them feeling that they would not remain guests forever. No one at all, really, until Bint Aamir returned from her failed trip, her visit to Dr. Thoms, and found herself facing the twins.

The Three Monkeys

Suroor led me to Kuhl, and there we were, three figures in a picture. The frame closed around us—Suroor, Kuhl, Zuhour—and did not let anyone else in. Then Suroor pushed one edge of the frame open and stepped outside the picture. But we remained three because Imran stepped in. Three figures in a picture, but now they were Zuhour, Kuhl, and Imran. We pulled the sides of the picture frame back together stubbornly, enclosing our triangle. We went along with our roles, while playing the game of exchanging places, and we didn't much pay attention to what we were doing. Or perhaps we did not want to pay attention.

Every morning when I woke up, the room was still dark, and my destiny waited for me. I would stare out at the breaking light and tell myself, "Dawn. It's another day." But my destiny had already come to pass. I walked right into it on my own two feet. The sides of the triangle were closed in on the three of us in a tight and perfect fit. I longed for every step I took, and I loathed every step I took, just as I longed for and was terrified by every obstacle along the way. I sat with

Kuhl and Imran in the Three Monkeys, my hands shaking
with the fear of abandonment and the dread of togetherness.
Every vein in my body pulsed with readiness, and every bit
of me was straining, on edge. *Waiting*: that word summed
up who I was. And this fate—which would not and could
not take any other course, which moved along the path that
I wished for fervently and feared terribly—was not in some
future, it was right here. It crouched on my back and I carried it wherever I might go. I covered it up beneath a lot of
talk about anything and everything. Everything but that fate
itself.

We were sitting together, on the café's patio, beneath the
open sky. I was longing to tell the two of them how much
I loved them. But I couldn't. I was frozen in my torment,
tongue-tied in my destiny. In the proximity of Imran's hair
so close to my fingers, in the tone of his skin, in Kuhl's dim-
ples, so prominent and rosy whenever she had the bliss of
being together with her beloved, the essence of this first and
elemental desire for union that eludes all description.

Kuhl was talking animatedly about her well-worked-
out graduation plans, and as usual, Imran was silent. I
couldn't pinpoint the source of his silence. Apprehension, or
indifference?

Looking at him, I could see the child he had been. Barefoot and hungry, coming out of his mud-brick home at dawn,

the green cotton boll splitting to reveal strands of cotton, and Imran bending to pick it carefully with his slim, precise fingers. He was not allowed to go to school through the whole of the cotton-harvest season, even when the cotton was not soft enough yet to be used for any purpose other than pillow stuffing or the heavy warp of rough blankets. A pair of fearsome eyes was always watching. There was a whip at the ready, and a red-hot iron spike with a sharp skewered end, and a bale of spiteful rancor that was beyond understanding. Even on the day his little sister was born, among heaps of cottonseed, he was not given permission to stop working in order to help his mother. He kept hearing her, the weak voice calling out for water, on and on until the sun went down and they all returned to the house, his father walking ahead, followed by him and his mother, clasping the newborn wrapped in a rag.

I finished my coffee. Suddenly Imran said that he hoped he would be able to visit my village. I invited him to come and see the bitter orange tree at our house, not telling him that it had died with my grandmother's death. Would these slim fingers, which had been rescued from the roughness of peasant farming, clasp the dried boughs of the dead bitter orange tree and return it to existence through the secret of this primary desire, this life-giving union? Will you swing, Imran, on the thick bough that was Sumayya's swing? Will you feel uncomfortable lying flat beneath the tree on a mat thin enough that under it you can feel the pebbles, Imran? But they are stones that speak, that breathe. You have to sit and swing your legs over the short branch of the bitter orange tree. You have to see the way the clouds fuse together and cling to the gray mountain peaks, and to call out my name, so that the peculiar echo resounds tens of times, as if strange, hidden creatures are holding your shout in their embrace, magnifying it. And you will know, then, that you seek to shout out the name of what is yours, and what must be there with you.

Miracles

In a place where people knew only traditional medicine until the late 1950s, news of Dr. Thoms's medical miracles reverberated through every grand palace, every house, every tent. Everywhere, people were talking about his operations—sewing up bellies, mending all sorts of fractures, and bringing the light back into eyes gone dark. The eye operation he performed on Imam Muhammad al-Khalili in Nizwa Town was a turning point: hearing of this success, people were newly ready to have faith in his modern medical miracles. The news revived their hopes of regaining the eyesight they'd lost to the excesses of ignorance and the lapses of neglect.

Bint Aamir undid her little cloth bundle. She unfolded the cloth with the crumpled brown rings whose color had faded, and extracted the silver anklet she had inherited from her mother and the gold earrings that Athurayyaa had given her one year when times were good. The cloth also enfolded the small Qur'an that she couldn't read, but which she had entrusted to Salman when he was about to go on the hajj, so that it would garner the blessings of Mecca; a glossy photograph of the Kaaba; a picture of Buraq, the blessed mount of Muhammad, with the face of a beautiful woman and the body of a horse; and a camel-bone writing tablet that dated all the way back to her brother's childhood, when he was a pupil at the village Qur'an school. The writing tablet was rescued from a fire in her father's house. A neighbor sent it to her—the same neighbor who told her, when she was aged twenty, that her father had rejected a man who presented himself as a suitor for her hand. She undid a small knot at the other end of her cloth and took out ten qirsh coins—her silver Maria Theresa thalers, earned from embroidering the trims on the sleeves of women's robes in the light of a kerosene flame in the evenings once Mansour had fallen asleep.

Her hand closed over five of the coins. She tied them back into the edge of her cloth and went to meet Bakhash, the owner of the Bedford truck that made the trip from Jaalaan to the Muscat region once a month, picking up people and goods along the way. Bakhash turned her down, saying his truck had filled up long before he reached her village and he still had a long road ahead, and many villages where he had to stop. But Bint Aamir wouldn't budge. She stood there in front of the vehicle while Bakhash and his aide, the oddly named Walad al-Kazz—who was also called al-Ma'yuni because that's what he was, a Super Helper—were piling sacks of rice, water tanks, and cartons of various goods onto the truck bed, stuffing them into every conceivable empty space. When they began hoisting the canisters of benzene, Bint Aamir picked up one herself. Bakhash yelled at her. "That's petrol, don't touch it! There are no petrol stations on the way." He snatched it from her. Near noon, when al-Ma'yuni went to the governor to secure a letter of permission to take the Bedford into the nearby villages, Bint Aamir followed close behind. The soles of her slippers had worn thin but she did not feel the sting of the hot stones. She stood at the threshold of the governor's residence until al-Ma'yuni came out with the military escort assigned to accompany—and watch— him. The two of them walked off and she followed behind. Finally Walad al-Kazz turned to her and said, "It's no use, you know. Bakhash isn't going to take you." She answered in a firm voice, "You take me." He cackled, his mouth opening enough that she could see his rotting teeth. "I'm just hired help. I load the thing, I haul up goods, I get permissions and I write down everyone's names, and I cook the meals. I make repairs, and I keep an eye on the tires." She answered him without so much as a faint smile. "Then you will write down my name." It annoyed him that even though she needed him, she didn't even bother to be nice. She didn't make any effort to feign astonishment at how many tasks he could do—why, he was the driver's aide, a cook, a mechanic, and a clerk. He swore to her—he'd divorce his wife if it wasn't true—that he could not convince Bakhash. That the list of people's names accompanied by the reasons they were traveling and could go into Muttrah was already settled, and that any trip on a large truck was difficult and uncomfortable and might even be dangerous. The truck would already be very heavy, and if they became mired in swampy ground, they would lose a whole day trying to get it out; and if they ran out of fuel, they would be stuck; and any passenger who rebelled against the conditions they were traveling in would be left on the side of the road. And if the governor of that region was irritated in any way, he would not give them a license to enter the town. When they reached the truck he pointed out the number hung on its side, and the letter *B* beside it, and he completed his tirade by asking, "Do you know what this is? Can you solve the puzzle? . . . It's a *B* for *barra. Outside.* The truck only has permission to stop outside Muscat. It can't go beyond *Derwazat al-Hatab*, and in case you didn't know, that's the enormous gate that leads into Muttrah City. You don't know, of course, that Sultan Sa'id bin Taymur imposes licenses on every single vehicle. If we wanted to sell this Bedford's license on the black market, we'd make more than the truck itself is worth. And then you come along and you think you can just put yourself in the middle of all these big important things, just because you want to get yourself to Muttrah or Muscat?" He was breathing hard, because of the heat but also because of the steady stare she was giving him. She undid the knot and pulled out the five silver coins.

"And I pay like anyone else does."

A little before sunset, Bakhash and al-Ma'yuni had finished loading and inspecting the truck, and the passengers who had been with them already were waiting to climb back in. The new passengers waited to have their names recorded. Bint Aamir stood at the back of the line. Walad al-Kazz whistled into her face in exasperation but he didn't dare throw her out. "Reason for travel?" he asked her. "Medical treatment with Thomas," she said firmly and clearly. She took her place in the truck next to a cage of live chickens that were to be slaughtered the next day for their midday meal.

Three days later, the Bedford arrived in Muttrah. It cleared the Gate of Tithes, where the taxes were imposed on all goods coming in or going out of the city. The truck joined others, coming from Sharjah, Dubai, and Fujayrah, all branded with the letter *B* to announce that they were not permitted beyond the Muttrah City boundary line. The list of passengers and their reasons for traveling here was dispatched, in order to procure permission to proceed. After that, the passengers were allowed to spread out to their respective destinations on condition that they meet exactly one week later in this exact spot in Derwazat al-Hatab.

The farmers hurried off to sell their harvest of dates and

dried lemons to the big merchants, who would repack them for export to India. The shop owners sped to the Muttrah suq to buy stock for their shops back in the remote villages: rice, coffee, spices, crates of tinned pineapple, mint breath-freshener lozenges, brightly colored fabric, and beads. The young men hurried off on their heroic attempts to travel to Bahrain for employment, or to Iraq for studies. But first they had to obtain that rare precious jewel: a passport, known as the Sa'idi passport because Sultan Sa'id had to agree person-ally to its being issued. The men and women who had gotten places on the truck because they needed treatment hurried to the missionary hospital in Muttrah, which eventually, after a decade or so of existence, came to be called al-Rahma, the Mercy Hospital.

Dr. Wells Thoms treated around eighty patients every day. Among them, on this day, my grandmother stood, taller than most, erect in her thirty-nine years, waiting for her name to be called. They told her that first she would see the Khatun. She was ushered into a room where a blond woman in a white uniform stood. "Are you the Khatun?" my grandmother asked. The American woman smiled and said sweetly, "My name is Beth Thoms." Her smile and her voice gave my grandmother a sense that the miracle must finally be near, for this was the famous doctor's wife. Beth gave her a printed, loose-bound book which my grandmother took with both hands as though she were receiving a divine gift. She did not tell the blond lady that she could not read or write. Or that this book—which she later learned was the Gospels—was only the second book she had ever held in her life, the first having been the Qur'an. Once home, she would place it among her treasured belongings as a memento of her meeting with Thomas.

My grandmother met Dr. Thoms like a lowly mortal meeting a saint or a holy man or a revered miracle worker who had turned people's dreams into reality. But it was a short appointment they had. This famous missionary doctor, who had performed the successful operation on the eye of the imam only a few years before, took only two minutes to examine my half-blind grandmother's eye before he informed her that the harm caused by the herbal treatments of her childhood was irredeemable, and no light would ever shine from this eye again. The nurse made a motion to conduct her out, but she refused to go. The doctor felt for her. He gave her a card on which he wrote her name, his diagnosis, and his prescription for antiseptic eye drops.

When I was on the threshold of twenty, on the threshold of traveling, impatient to follow my path, on a buoyant tide of confidence in life and brimming with plans and desires; when my grandmother was dying, and I was collecting her clothes and her few, simple belongings, packing them before taking her to the hospital, I came upon this card, and I read the print on the back, a line from the biblical book of Proverbs. FEAR OF THE LORD IS THE BEGINNING OF WISDOM.

A judge who had been among the passengers tried to delay their return trip. It seems he was still hoping against hope, despite the letter with its official seal that he had stuffed inside his clothing. But Bakhash and Walad al-Kazz would not hear of it; they held to the time they had set for the truck's departure. And so the judge had to take his place meekly among the sacks of coffee and the tins of jelly sweets. Humiliated, he was making every effort not to meet anyone's eyes, for these villagers were all witness to his disgrace, even if indirectly. The qirsh coins filling his cloth bag to the point where its seams were straining could not prevent his slide from grace. Those coins were lucre amassed through his many years as a judge working to further the interests of Sultan Sa'id bin Taymur, including coins acquired from selling the many baskets of eggs and cages of chickens that those he had judged guilty dispatched to his home during the night, hoping he would give them light sentences. No, in spite of his bulging bag and the metallic thud of one coin against another, he had not managed to find a cure for his ailing eye. Thoms told him flatly that it could not be treated anywhere in the region of Muscat. If he were to travel to Bombay, on the other hand, he would find options for treatment there. It was possible to have an operation there that might save the eye. The judge was nonplussed. True, his long-practiced facility with the art of bribery meant he had a bag of money that could carry him to Bombay. But there was one problem. He needed a passport. To go to India, he needed permission from the sultan. The judge wrote a letter to the sultan, explaining his circumstances. He had *all* the money that might be necessary, his letter intimated. The only thing lacking was the passport—and the permission needed to secure it. The response came immediately, with bureaucratic efficiency and brevity, and with the signature of Sultan Saʿid bin Taymur himself, along with his seal. The sultan was hardly blind to the judge's ways. "No permission to travel granted. We are confident that one eye will be adequate to your needs until the moment of your death."

On the return trip, al-Maʿyuni's throat opened in song. All the way home, they were nourished by dates and dried shark. They got out at the Muqayhafa well for a rest break shaded by a lotus tree, and he urged them to have a good, long drink. One of the women whispered to the other women that as she had napped, on the way, she saw her child in a dream, garlanded in jasmine. She had left the nursing infant at home. Bint Aamir's good eye teared up. The dream told her that the newborn had died and was already buried in the ground.

War

Bint Aamir came back to the home of Salman and Athurayyaa after the longest trip she had ever taken in her life, this journey to see Dr. Thoms. As she entered, she noticed two pairs of wooden clogs lined up carefully at the threshold of the reception room, which opened onto the courtyard by means of an archway. She was puzzled, and the sight of those clogs left her feeling uneasy. She pulled off her ragged footwear and called for Mansour, wanting to give him the little hoard of milk chocolate she had bought for a half-qirsh at the Muttrah suq. But instead, in response she heard an unfamiliar, high-pitched voice. "Mansour isn't here."

She did not move. It was her first encounter, face-to-face, with this pair who would fast become her adversaries. Two thin, feeble-looking women emerged from somewhere inside. As if twenty years had not passed since they boarded the ship to Africa, Bint Aamir knew immediately who they were. Already, sweat was pouring from her face. The blazing midday heat felt like a brutal slap. She was almost gasping for breath, as she stood there clutching the little bag of milk chocolate. But the severe heat did not keep her from noticing the hard, determined flare in the eyes of Rayyaa and Raayah. She noticed the leopard skin, too, which now hung on the wall. It was all perfectly clear, without need for a word of explanation. This was war.

The three women stood still and silent in the reception room of Salman's house: Bint Aamir towering and rigid, the perspiration gleaming on her brow; Rayyaa, her sickly thinness accentuated by the hump swelling and rounding her back; and Raayah, so strikingly skeletal that she appeared almost weaker, even, than her feeble-looking sister. Her eyes were half-obscured by a thing Bint Aamir now saw for the very first time: prescription eyeglasses. The leopard skin looked down on them, witness to their battles, from this first one on to later triumphs and defeats. That leopard skin was arbiter of every advance and every retreat.

The sisters inched forward cautiously. They greeted Bint Aamir formally. Bint Aamir said nothing. Her response, instead, was to dive straightaway into the whirlwind of activity that was her accustomed life. The sisters slipped along on the fringes of this storm. The first thing that Bint Aamir did, upon her return, was to fill with dirt the nests of scorpions Mansour had worked hard to maintain and tend all the while she was away. Next, she strode to the falaj, walking back balancing on her head the big clay jugs filled with water for cooking. Then she cleaned and washed the rice, slaughtered a rooster, and made the midday meal. When she set it all out on a cloth on the floor, Rayyaa and Raayah emerged again, to gather around it with Salman, Athurayyaa, and Mansour. On that particular day, Bint Aamir did not eat. She was remembering her father, slapping her brother's hand so hard that the grains of rice he was bringing to his mouth flew in every direction. She sniffed at the air, heavy with the smell of wet dirt after rainfall, and silently she repeated the words that had expelled the two of them from her father's care: "Eat from the toil of your own arm!"

The war broke out, silent but fierce. Bint Aamir set the limits of the sisters' movements through the household. She did not allow them to enter her kitchen, or to touch her trees, which she had planted and had kept alive with her constant care. They were never to criticize or chide Mansour, her son. Ever. Rayyaa and Raayah responded by trotting out their perfumed clothes and making certain that the clip-clip of their fine wooden clogs was heard constantly. They told endless stories about Africa—rain forests and grasslands, leopards and rituals, gigantic snakes and long grasses, domed houses . . . Their vivid narratives held the attention of Salman and Athurayyaa, Mansour and the neighborhood women.

The silent war could have gone on for a very long time.

But the twins' life in the Congo had taught them not to wait for attention from whatever body in God's creation might chance to offer it. They could not have been in that household for much more than two weeks before they began searching out the haphazard pile of mud bricks in which they had spent their childhood. They were quick to see that the drought had receded from the villages and hamlets; the barrenness they remembered vaguely from childhood was no more. Once again, the falaj was pouring water into the orchards. They began working to strengthen their ties with the women living nearby, who volunteered to teach them sewing and helped to spread the word that these twins were available for hire to fast as substitutes for those who could not do so themselves, or for those who wanted to employ them to fast as an act of atonement in memory of a dearly departed one.

On this particular morning, Bint Aamir was washing Mansour's clothes. She slapped them hard against the wide stone edge of the falaj, and plunged them into the water again. She repeated her actions again and again, and not until she was convinced that the garments were pure clean and no longer held any traces of the pungent smell redolent of an adolescent boy did she squeeze out the water and hang the clothes to dry on the palm-fiber rope. She was completely absorbed in her laundry when the twins came to stand over her bent head. Straightening her eyeglasses over her nose,

Raayah said, "We came to say goodbye, Bint Aamir. We're leaving Salman's home for our home." Our: a swift and sure arrow, guaranteed to put a puncture wound in Bint Aamir's chest.

Rayyaa and Raayah had made plans to transform the dilapidated dwelling into a one-room sheltered space suitable for habitation. They figured out how to redirect the course of the falaj so that it would water their dead little orchard. Putting together all the money they had made from fasting on others' behalf and the coins they made from sewing, they bought the mud brick they needed to repair the walls, and then the palm seedlings to populate the orchard. Neither Rayyaa's lump nor Raayah's weak eyesight kept them from working night and day. They finished building the room in one corner of the collapsed old house, and that was enough for them. They planted bananas and mangoes and tomatoes, lemon trees, onions, and clover in addition to the palm trees. Within two years they had a cow that gave them milk. They sold that milk, and samna and cheese; they continued to take in sewing and to fast for hire. They made an independent life.

"Ma sha Allah!" you could hear the women exclaim to one another. "Rayyaa and Raayah work like men and they don't need anyone." Envy tormented my grandmother, even though she had always been extremely wary of its scorching flames and considered it the worst of all possible sins. When people described the twins as independent, my grandmother muttered to herself, "Yes, and how proud they have let themselves be!" Her dream of having a plot of land and living from it—from her own earnings—had come to an end, just as earlier, her dream of having one perfectly sound eye had ended, too.

A Good-Enough Excuse

After Saddam invaded Kuwait, my father bought such huge quantities of basic foodstuffs, even though he did not have enough space for all of it in the storeroom. He put the sacks of rice in my grandmother's room. Seeing her bumping into the sacks and stumbling, we could guess that only a tiny amount of light remained in her one working eye. By the time the war was over and the sacks had disappeared, and my father went back to his long commercial excursions, my grandmother was so lame that she could no longer get around. Once, between trips, my father saw her dragging her body from her room to the shade of the bitter orange tree. He said only one word. "Maah."

My grandmother smiled. "Mansour."

That was when my father bought the wheelchair. My grandmother never used it. He hired someone to come and help. My grandmother would not allow the woman to help with bathing. Not even once. Then those years of strangeness dissolved into something else.

My suitcase was packed for travel, ready to depart for my life as a student overseas.

Sumayya's cases were packed for the wedding, ready to escort her as she embraced her new bliss and the move to her husband's home.

Sufyan had barely said goodbye to his childhood, but he was packing it away and entering the perils of adolescence.

My grandmother died.

The people around me were sympathetic, but no one was prepared to understand me. Sympathy isn't understanding. Mostly, I think, it takes an opposite road. "Aah, she was over eighty, after all." "Aah, now she is at rest from the pain." "Now, you know, she no longer has to crawl from her room to the courtyard. She's somewhere much better." "Aah, you all took such good care of her."

Isn't old age a good-enough excuse for dying? Or, more important, a good-enough excuse for accepting the death of someone we love? That's what people think, I suppose. Just as my grandmother was fortunate enough to receive a lot of sympathy in her life, or at least some, I was fortunate enough to receive it when she died. But neither of us was fortunate enough to have true understanding come our way. And I wasn't allowed to have, or supposed to have, such powerful feelings of regret pulsing through me.

Sumayya the Dynamo got married, and then she lost her

title and became just Sumayya. And then I went away. And then all those hours passed, all those years, which we managed to fling away, conveniently forgetting what had opened our wounds in the first place; forgetting how to diagnose the causes. But we did sometimes remind ourselves that those wounds had not gone away. Because after all, at some point in time—even before the passage of those hours and years— we had already been broken into pieces.

The fragile bird of life took us along. We clung to its wings so hard that they dissolved in our grip; and so we tried to put those feathers on ourselves. We dressed ourselves in those feathers, and we drank the blood of that bird we had destroyed, and we told ourselves, "We will go on." We kept saying that, even as the bird fell apart, ripped to pieces in our fingers, and as we had to endure the acrid taste of its blood beneath our tongues. "We will go on," we said. And then we waited expectantly for the bird of life to soar again into the sky, taking us with it. We waited and waited.

We clothed ourselves in affliction, in the vulnerable nakedness of our love. We opened our mouths to receive those drops of honey but what ran down our throats tasted bitter. We clung so fiercely to the beloved body that our fingernails tore the garments upon it to shreds, and that body, worn to tatters, weakened until it could no longer wrap our nakedness protectively in its own. The affliction was ours; our fingers, trying to pluck that love apart, sapped the beloved energies. The cries, ever louder, simply deafened us. Our attempts to run away left us lame. Our despair brought us low. And we asked, with Job: Why, O Lord, Most Merciful of the merciful, why in our affliction do you not see us, cleansed and drenched?

Eyeglasses

When she made her trip to see Dr. Thoms, Bint Aamir stayed in a roofed-over shelter erected close to the walls of Mercy Hospital. Many women crowded into that place, coming from all over, each paying a small fee to stay there and bringing her own food. Every midday, smoke rose from the single-burner gas cookers, and soon after sundown, the women were all falling asleep.

The men were jammed into an adjacent shelter. The woman who shared a bed with Bint Aamir tossed and turned and moaned, keeping Bint Aamir from sleeping. Bint Aamir gave her a little prod with her elbow. "Ya bint in-nas! What's wrong with you, girl? Let's try to get some sleep." The young woman started crying. "I want my husband. We came here a month ago for treatment and he's in the men's shelter and I'm in the women's. We only see each other at the hospital during the day."

Did my grandmother get any sleep that night?

Was her head full of thoughts, too? Maybe about the re-mote and unknown fiancé of whom she knew nothing, not even his name, this man whom her father had rejected with-out even sending for her, without even letting her know?

If the fiancé had become a husband and with him she had known the pleasures of the body, would she, too, have been restless with longing, as this young woman was?

Rayyaa and Raayah left her a pair of clogs as a gift before they left for their decrepit home and their dead orchard. But my grandmother did not touch them. She left the clogs at the threshold where the twins had set them down, and she went on wearing her worn-thin slippers. She preferred binding palm fibers to the soles of her feet to touching those clogs.

She ignored the clogs, but she kept thinking about the eyeglasses for months. She even thought about putting her-self out to fast for hire, so that she could put together enough money to buy a pair of eyeglasses. Surely, any of their ac-quaintances who were traveling to the city would be able to pick them up for her. She didn't have the slightest idea about ordering eyeglasses, no sense that you had to have your sight examined. But in any case, her body could not endure long fasts: it could barely carry itself through the obligatory fasts the length of the month of Ramadan and on the two holy days of Arafah and Ashura. She found it so hard that she took pity on Mansour when his father first ordered him to fast. That year, she spent the first day of Mansour's first Ra-madan fast pouring water over his head and body, trying to keep the heat away and hoping to lessen his thirst. But on his own, Mansour came up with a handy trick. It was just a little ruse dappled with innocence, which Mansour discovered by lying down at midday directly beneath the date palm where there hung a small jahla.

Throughout the entire month, promptly at midday, Mansour was there, staring up at the drops of water collecting on the surface of the clay jahla. He watched as the little drops gradually came together as one large drop rolling down the side of the clay pitcher. That's when he opened his mouth, still lying there perfectly positioned below, until that rich, perfect drop plopped into his mouth. He would continue his vigil, reckoning the exact timing, until the second drop fell into his open mouth. When his father grew suspicious about Mansour's sudden love of lying beneath the jahla through the hottest moments of the day, the boy managed to escape the paternal whip by insisting that he had not broken the fast. A drop fell into his insides by accident! It must have been a boon from God, and so God meant him to have this blessed sustenance!

My grandmother knew that she would not have the strength to fast for pay. But she wanted those eyeglasses.

I press my cheek into the pillow. Snowflakes are flying into the windowpane. I press my cheek down harder, until the pillow forces my right eye closed. My left eye stays open.

I form the word *awraa* on my lips and it circles and circles through my head. One-eyed. I move the letters around and try other combinations. I try to imagine how someone could live for eighty years with only one eye. The tears run from my eyes, from both my eyes, from my two sound eyes. My tears spill over her one eye, which is damaged; over the herbal concoctions that were prescribed by ignorance; over the violence and harshness of childhood; over children orphaned by their mothers' deaths and thrown out by their fathers, and over their brothers' tragic ends; over a field she did not possess; over a companion she was never fortunate enough to have; over a son who is not hers; over the grandchildren of a friend who died before she did.

A Yellow Rain from India

Salman died twice. The first time was when some sailors in torn robes and bare feet, colored rags binding their heads, knocked on the door to Salman's home and informed Athurayyaa that on the way to India, the ship had foundered on the coast near Bombay. No one had escaped alive.

Salman had traveled to India two or three times before, with cargoes of dried dates that he had worked long days and nights to harvest and prepare. They boiled the dates in huge vats over a constantly replenished supply of wood, the hissing of the boiling water sending terror into the children gathered around, waiting for the water to be poured off and the dates to be lifted out to dry in the sun. The children were paid twenty bisa for every reed mat they could cover with dates, lining them up carefully so that the sun would reach each individual date. It was an annual ritual and a bit of a party as well. Salman's keen involvement extended to accompanying this export to India himself. But it wasn't just about the dates. Every time, he came back with a pile of books for Athurayya: legendary exploits and biographies and the ancient reports of the pious ancestors' lives and deeds. He had also acquired high-quality silks, gold-embroidered cushions, ornately fashioned wooden boxes, finely worked silver kohl pots, spices, and tea. He expanded his shop, and his commerce.

When the sailors left Athurayya on that day, the skies opened and a yellow rain pelted down. Athurayyaa put on white mourning clothes for the third time in her life. But this time, and for the first time, when all the mirrors in the house were covered by heavy black fabric, it was because this was what she wanted. But still, she could not put to rest a sense of bewilderment and denial. In fact, she found it harder and harder to believe the news that Salman had died; that he had drowned and might well be lying inside the belly of a whale or a large fish. Less than a month later, Salman himself came back, loaded down with his precious mercantile goods. He opened up his shop, to the light, to laughter, and to new goods. Athurayyaa peeled off her mourning clothes as if she had emerged from an oppressive nightmare and said to him, "I knew you were still alive."

But he died a second time. The relative who had gone with him to Bombay so that Salman could seek treatment for respiratory problems came back to tell the widow that he had buried Salman with his own hands in the Muslims' cemetery there. The Indian physicians had been unsuccessful in treating him. His heart, which had held nothing but love for Athurayyaa, had erupted. In the final moments of his life, he had her image before him, exactly as he had first seen her when he came back from Zanzibar: a young woman with fright in her eyes, a look that made him dizzy with desire to answer her needs, and hands that had never been scratched or scarred. A very young woman who had buried a son and two husbands before she learned how to braid her own hair.

This time, the certainty of his death was a lance that settled directly in her heart, burying itself deeper and deeper until her heart erupted just as his had. This time, Athurayyaa felt the same sense of shyness and innocent shame that had paralyzed her on the day she married him; the shyness that propelled her to believe that she did not deserve this gift, that it was no longer suitable for her to joyously celebrate a wedding, to want to make herself pretty, to marry, once she had put two husbands in the ground. When Salman died for the second time, she felt this same onrush of guilty innocence, and that is what convinced her that he was truly dead. This time, her sense of embarrassment welled up because she was still alive—she was breathing air and tasting food and walking among the living. It was then that she felt it was no longer right, no longer suitable, for her to live, to go on, to pick up the petty little matters of life on this earth. And so the sharp arrow edge of certainty that Salman was dead wound deep into her heart, further and further, slowly but determinedly. Deeper and deeper, until her heart erupted and died. In less than a year, she followed him.

After Athurayyaa died, she was wrapped in the length of fine cloth that her daughter, Hasina, had sent home while still a bride: a gift from Burundi, along with her first letter to her mother. The color had faded even though Athurayyaa had never touched that fabric. She had always waited for the moment when her child would return to her embrace; only then would she drape that beautiful length of fabric over her body. As it happened, though, the moment never came, and the one instruction she ever gave about this cloth was that it was the only shroud she would wear after her death.

Perfection

We were in the meadow just next to the university buildings. Flocks of birds were gathering, about to make their long winter migration. We hugged our heavy coats around us and gripped our paper cups, full of hot coffee. "I don't see what the problem is!" Christine exclaimed to Kuhl. "You love Imran, so marry him for real. Your parents love you, they'll understand." As she spoke, Christine was all but hopping from foot to foot. It was impossible to imagine her speech or her wiry figure unaccompanied by this constant, energetic movement. As impossible as imagining Kuhl without this look in her eyes—lost in love—and her dreamy smile.

Kuhl gripped Christine's arm. "Christine . . . they won't understand."

Christine shook her head vigorously, riffling her blond hair, now cut short. "Maybe if you come clean with your mother first."

Kuhl laughed drily. "My mother? When I decided, along

with Suroor, to start wearing hijab, she refused to be seen with us. We couldn't go to any theaters or restaurants with her, because her friends might see us."

"You have to be perfect in your mother's eyes." My words were barely audible.

"Uuh. The contemporary mother!" said Kuhl. "Her child is the one who ends up with all the responsibility for keeping her happy, and not frustrating her hopes and plans. Because everything was all planned out for that child from the moment of birth or before."

"And swerving off the path of the maternal plan is unforgiveable?" asked Christine.

"Yes." Kuhl's voice was firm. "Because what kept our grandmothers busy, all the time, totally, was just keeping their children alive, keeping them safe as best they could, given the conditions they lived in, the poor medical care and all. What keeps today's mother busy is inserting her child into the agenda."

So that's why grandmothers didn't have such a sense of guilt, I mused out loud. And why they were more accepting of children who were always ill or had some imperfection, as they saw it, or didn't seem very intelligent.

Kuhl laughed again, her laugh thin and bitter. "But our mothers—ours—search for perfection in us, because we came into their world according to a carefully drawn plan where there were no uncertainties lurking. And we will be even harsher than they are in these matters."

"Well, personally," said Christine, "my dreams are limited to having one kid, no more than that."

We answered in one voice. "Planning the kid already."

"But really." Christine was musing. "Do you really think I wouldn't let my own child do something that went against my thinking?"

"Of course you wouldn't!" said Kuhl. "Just like my mother, who won't let me do anything that frustrates her dreams, which means marrying me into a family higher up on the social scale than my family is, or at least into one that's as elite as ours."

We occupied ourselves with staring at the birds, in silence. Had Sumayya frustrated my mother's dreams when she stopped talking to anyone—to anyone at all—after her husband died by drowning?

The blessing of happiness, the peace of good conscience, were forever destroyed for Sumayya the Dynamo. The blessing of contentment and acceptance had been forever destroyed for my mother by the nervous attacks that followed each of her miscarriages. After Sumayya was widowed and went silent, my mother went back to wandering through the rooms of the house at night, unable to sleep, exactly as she had done after Sufyan's birth.

She could not bear Sumayya's silence. She could not bear that this young daughter of hers had become a widow in such tragic circumstances. And then! How was it possible, then—how dared she?—lose her voice, withdraw from the power of words? This was too much.

In that moment, observing Kuhl's twisted smile, I thought about what it must be, to be a mother like mine. To give birth only to three children, none of whom ever came close to perfection.

The Theater

After graduating from King's College London, Kuhl's mother tried to get work in theater production. She actually secured two or three meetings with Hanif Kureishi, for the purpose of presenting her ideas. She believed he would help her, because, she said, "All of those in London with Pakistani roots must help each other out, of course they must." That's what she had heard her father say repeatedly. But Kuhl's mother stumbled, with her expectations of help as well as her understanding of theater itself. She tried to make up for this by frequently attending plays and cocktail parties hosted by former classmates for whom the stage curtains had graciously parted more than they had for her. She had her special soiree attire, black and bare-backed, with her black hair left loose and flowing. She took great care to never appear fatigued even after hours in high heels, resembling—unconsciously—one character or another in a Hanif Kureishi play.

At one such party she met a very gallant and good-looking man, who was in London to wed some serious money to works of art. Unlike her, he was not a Londoner. He lived in Karachi, where he ran Pakistan's leading bank. This attractive young woman had already let go of her theatrical ambitions by then, and she was ready to accept his offer of marriage, on condition that he buy her a flat in London where she could spend the summers. Her other condition was that he would not force her to have children. The banker complied, and two weddings were held: one in London in a white gown, and one in Karachi in red Punjabi.

After three happy and carefree years, however, the still-young bride realized that the only way she would ever strengthen her position in her husband's family would be through the sanctified status of mother. And so she planned it all out, following the prescriptions that were supposed to guarantee that she would have a male child and heir. But when the child came, it was a girl. And three years later, when she tried again, another girl. If she didn't stop now, she thought, this stream would become a torrent and the undercurrent would submerge her. It could destroy her figure and demolish her freedom, and it might even put an end to her husband's affectionate coddling. Suroor and Kuhl were enough, she decided. She would make do with them.

The older Kuhl got, the more her mother's disappointment with the fruits of her own motherhood grew. Who would ever believe that this daughter, with her brittle, frail hair and irregular features and rather too full body, was her daughter? *Her* daughter! She for whom marriage and child-bearing had only enhanced her bewitching magic, her elegance, her shine! Kuhl's mother dismissed her daughter's intelligence and success, and preferred Kuhl's younger sister, Suroor—so pretty, so subdued, so perfect! Their mother made her preference obvious in so many ways.

The envy and anger that could have erupted so easily between the sisters did not appear. Kuhl withdrew into her own world, creating a place for herself. Suroor showed her respect and affection, but mixed with strong sentiments of guilt, as though she had to atone for being regarded as prettier and more delicate and perhaps more refined. And for having a bigger piece of her mother's heart, which could not expand to embrace someone so unlike herself.

My mother? She never preferred one of us over another. But maybe she never liked any of us very much. My grandmother Bint Aamir was the one who cared. She was the one who handled everything we needed, and she was sternly equal in her attentions. Or maybe, perhaps, did she love Sufyan best? I don't remember. Anyway, the difference in our ages, the six years between us, erased any threat of jealousy. Instead, my eyes were glued to the wall, where Sumayya eternally hung suspended in time.

The Snowman, and the Man of Ice

Suroor stepped outside our triangle because I could no longer go along with her discomfort. I knew that her feelings were based on perfectly understandable moral principles, an anger that stemmed from the errors of other people, the irritation felt by those who are perfect with those who lack their perfection, or rather, against those who persist in their imperfect ways, and continue making their mistakes. Specifically, the errors of her sister, Kuhl. Sins and errors of passion: that was not something for which one could be absolved.

Before Suroor stepped out of this trio we had made, she told me that Imran was like dried grass, a brittle, fragile, but stubborn stalk clinging to a marble column, and that no matter how stubborn the stalk, fragility would in the end prevail, breaking down that obstinate loyalty. The stalk would not be able to hold on; against that marble column it would break or crumple, the wind carrying it off like any ordinary, ephemeral twig. And with that, Suroor pushed aside one rib of the triangle with her thin, elegant fingers—fingers that would never be set on fire by the touch of a lover—and walked out.

She did not even turn back for a single look. And then Imran, so very thin and yet as different as could be from a flimsy length of straw, soon replaced the side of the triangle that had been pulled away. Kuhl had hinted once about what she saw as the rather limited attention he paid to other people, but I came to see things very differently.

In Lahore, on the only school trip he ever took out of his remote village, he saw the way the skyline seemed to blend into the towers on either side of the old castle's gate, and it left a permanent mark in his mind. He tried to draw his classmates' attention to this singular and powerful impression, but he soon realized that they could only react to tangible objects, while his sensibility stretched further. For the first time, he sensed that at the very base and core of this world was a tiny aperture through which time itself crept. His sarcastic classmates made fun of him when he tried seriously to explain this notion of time's prodigious, yet tiny, puncture in the universe. From that moment on, he made every effort to conceal what he really thought and felt, and he worked to develop means of self-defense against the ability of human beings to hurt other human beings.

I put my hand out to Imran, and I saw my thumb disfigured and black. I thought I stepped toward him but I found myself almost leaping, trying to span a much vaster distance. I realized uncomfortably that I was fleeing the sound of my grandmother calling out, her voice coming thinly from the isolation of her room. I found that my head was spinning on the ice. My head collided with Imran's chest. But his chest was carved from stone and it shattered my head into slivers that landed on the street. The children were picking up these ice shards, and trying to make a snowman. I saw my eyes in his icy eyes. I saw my shattered nose in the snowman's carrot nose.

I was spending whole evenings here just staring out at the ice and snow. I would phone home, to speak to my mother and father and Sufyan, and I always sent my affectionate greetings to Sumayya. One time, my mother handed the phone to her, but Sumayya would not say a word, which in turn stopped me from saying anything. It was a conversation I didn't know how to start. It was up to her to say something. Anything at all, some nonsense like: "Mrs. Hiba is a fat, burned loaf of bread!" Or something from the past like: "Stab Fattoum with a pencil if she tries to attack you." Or, "Don't scream the way you did at my grandmother's funeral." Or, "Watch out that the boys don't destroy the brown lizards' graves, otherwise their tails will turn into whips and they'll come after us." Or even, "If the spiny-tailed lizard pounces, it will cling to us and it won't let go until seven cows

in the heavens and seven cows on earth are lowing." Or, "Get
Gran to understand that Samira Sa'id isn't Samira Tawfiq."
Or, "You take the bread to Gran. I have other things to do."
But she didn't say any such thing. She didn't say a word. So I
was silent. My mother took the receiver and ended the call.

It was Sumayya who taught me to slink into the kitchen
at noon to mix powdered milk with sugar and then to creep
away with a fistful of the delightful mix. It was Sumayya who
warned me against ever admitting that I hadn't memorized
the poems we were supposed to learn for our class in oral
recitation. It was Sumayya who taught me to always take
a seat at the very end of the very last row, so that I could
memorize the lesson by listening to all the other girls who
had to recite before I did. Sumayya tutored me on how to
say *ayy luf yuu* to the blond son of the English teacher. At
home, Sumayya got me to put on a performance, insisting
that I really did need an increase in my allowance in order to
buy colored pencils for drawing class—so that she could take
the money and buy Mustafa Qamar's latest cassette tapes.
Together, we glued the chicken feathers onto Sufyan's back
and pretended we were going to throw him from the top of
the wall so that we could see him fly, all because we wanted
our mother to see us and be so frightened that she would
actually dash across the courtyard without putting her shoes
on first. Sumayya shouted, "Look at elegant Lady Merchant's

Daughter running barefoot in the dirt!" We tossed Sufyan into my father's arms, and then my father chased us with a whip.

We had a lot of confidence in life (now I would add under my breath, "more than we should have had"). Confidence in our youth, our pleasures, the paths we were taking, our house and home. Confidence that the word *broken* did not exist. We walked through the streets hand in hand as if our interlaced fingers could be undone by nothing short of death. And death was a mere shadow, a remote thing somewhere out there. There was no cause to dent our happiness by thinking about it. The house was ours; it never crossed our minds that there could be any possibility of losing it. Sofas and beds and pillows and windows and doorknobs and the Sony cassette player and school bags—it all belonged to us. We didn't feel a moment's uncertainty about anything. To press our cheeks down against the old carpet in the sitting room in an attempt to imagine the kings of the jinn perched on the chandeliers above: that was what happiness meant.

And we had the trees my grandmother had planted in the garden, we had shoots growing in pots, clothes hanging on hangers, opened letters sitting in drawers, spoons and forks and knives and plates on the kitchen shelves. We had my mother's fragility, and my grandmother's fierce will; my father bringing us gifts from his travels, and Sufyan's amusing little bouts of troublemaking. All of it was ours, and we didn't doubt that for a moment. We didn't ask, not even once, whether we were right or wrong to think as we did. What we had was certainty and contentment and pleasure in life. As far as we knew, no dictionaries yet included the word *broken*, let alone multiple definitions for it.

We did not cross out the days on the calendar hanging on the wall. We did not turn the pages, we did not keep old newspapers, or add new sections to our picture albums, or hang old photographs on the walls. We did not save up our smiles or our dance steps for a later time when we might need them. We did not count the glasses of tea or the cups of coffee we drank.

Talisman

A fever attacked Imran. Fright and Kuhl both held me tightly.

After some hesitation and a lot of thinking about arguments for and against, we decided to visit him in his tiny flat. It wasn't an easy decision, since he shared it with five other Pakistani male students. "We'll say we are his relatives," said Kuhl. But no one asked us.

There was no lift in the building. The ground floor was occupied by an ancient pub. We walked up the four flights in silence, Kuhl leading the way. We stopped in front of the door to the flat, unsure of ourselves. Kuhl adjusted her hijab. "We'll say we are his relatives," she said again.

We knocked. A tall young man wearing iPod earbuds opened the door. Kuhl greeted him in Urdu, but he couldn't hear her. He stepped aside to let us in, leaving the door open. Kuhl and I stood there in the middle of the sitting room. There were articles of clothing everywhere, and empty pizza boxes piled up on the table along with some open cans of soda. The young man waved at the room to the right. We went in.

Kuhl walked steadily over to the bed where Imran was lying. I remained in the doorway. She leaned over him and gave him an awkward, tearful embrace. I felt a shiver go through me. This portrait had been drawn when I was still outside the picture frame. This love belonged to the two of them; I was simply there on its threshold. A witness, but also there to be witnessed, the onlooker who gave the picture a surround: an outside. The picture frame left no fuzzy boundaries: it wrapped firmly around a pair of lovers in an embrace. Like an artist's sketching pencil about to attempt a crude first draft, I was immobile, unsure. I stood there in the doorway, on the threshold, without any ground to stand on, without any colors to add to this picture. I was lost in this little room where Imran's fever seemed to hike the air temperature upward. A curtain of colored beads hung between the room and a dark passageway that must lead to the bathroom; every now and then, a faint light coming from within fell on the beads, producing flashes of color as it bounced off. On the wall behind the bed hung a big poster of the cricket star Imran Khan. I had no idea whether or not our Imran was a cricket fan.

His clothes hung in a plastic wardrobe, the collapsible kind, neatly and carefully organized. There seemed no connection whatsoever between his very orderly room and the living room, as if his room had been set down in this flat by mistake. I wanted to put my hand out to touch Imran's shirts, to run my fingers along the buttons and the spaces between, where Kuhl had said her spirit clung. The small table held a neat stack of very big books on top of which sat a stethoscope. I imagined Imran listening to my heartbeat, the two of us laughing as if we were playing a silly game. Then I heard his voice calling me. So he had noticed I was here. I went closer to him. To them. "Hi, Imran. How are you? I hope you are feeling better." His eyes lit up for a moment and he smiled weakly, half sitting up and then leaning back. He was wearing a white undershirt. Drops of sweat ran down his neck. My hands ached to reach out and wipe away the dampness, but Kuhl's fingers were already there.

As her hand rubbed his neck gently and the drops of sweat vanished, the image filled my mind. I loved this—seeing her hand caressing his neck. I wanted Kuhl's hand to stay there, and I wanted to go on staring at this picture, on and on. He was a peasant, he said, as strong as an ox, and he would get better quickly. Kuhl laughed as she brushed tears from her eyes, and the veins in his temples pulsed. Her eyelids trembled open and shut. My heart fluttered like the wings of a bird beating at the air.

Kuhl knelt down at Imran's head, chatting away, and I stood at his feet. Everything about her was lovable. Imran looked at her and then at me, back and forth. The light in the room was low; it was an overcast day. But the glow in Imran's eyes as he looked at me lit the whole room and inflamed my chest. I could feel his sweat running down my neck, and Kuhl's tears running down my cheeks. I could hear the soil of farm fields—the fields Imran had worked, the plot my grandmother dreamed of—in Kuhl's throaty laugh. I could see the strength and health there, behind his quizzical smile. He asked me to go and fetch us some juice from the kitchen, just asked simply and straightforwardly, like someone making a request of his sister, or of his wife.

I tried to find some glasses but I was defeated by the chaos in the kitchen. I opened a cupboard and saw a stack of small, shiny colored bowls. What a familiar sight! The long-ago memory made me smile.

Our neighbor Shaykha had complained time after time that her plastic dishware, which she would wash by sitting on the edge of the falaj and dipping each bowl in, was disappearing. By the time she would have finished washing the rest of the kitchen things, the little bowls would have vanished. She would have to return home carrying the basin of kitchenware but without her shiny plastic bowls.

Sumayya decided to form the Sherlock Holmes Detachment for Solving the Mystery of the Missing Bowls—chief detective, Sumayya. She assigned me the duty of watching the area to the right of the canal, while Sumayya kept her eyes on the left side. We soon discovered that Fattoum was stealing the plastic bowls, and we followed her. She descended to the falaj's first ford, where the women swam, concealed from onlookers by the simple roofed structure there. In the darkness and emptiness there, and in every ford above it, Fattoum dropped her excrement into a bowl and set it on the water, to be dragged by the current to the next ford, where a woman engrossed in her bathing would scream at the disgusting sight.

Sumayya caught Fattoum in the act. Shaykha hit Fattoum over and over with the thick rubber soles of her flip-flops. The Sherlock Holmes Detachment succeeded in its mission, but that was the day on which I fell into the clutches of Fattoum and her brother, Ulyan, who punished me whenever they found me alone, without Sumayya. They discovered my weak point easily: it was my hair. Ulyan yanked at my hair viciously while Fattoum slapped me and rubbed dirt into it. I was never able to mount a successful resistance, until the day when my grandmother threatened them and I was delivered from danger.

I came back from the kitchen with the pineapple juice that Kuhl loved. Her face was beaming now. Had Imran deliberately sent me out of the room so that he could kiss her?

"Just imagine," said Kuhl merrily. "His eminence the doctor won't take any medication." Imran smiled, animating his already attractive face to which the fever had given a noticeable sheen. I teased them. "You doctors, all of you—you won't practice what you preach!"

"My mother always fought fevers by hanging amulets around my neck," said Imran. I pulled up the one chair in the room and sat facing them. Now we did form a triangle. I began to tell them the story.

I was nine years old, and weak with fever. My father took me to the clinic and we came back with a strip of pills that didn't have any effect. It seems I began to babble, and my mother broke out in sobs. My father led her away to her own bed and called out for his mother Bint Aamir to stay up with me and nurse me. My grandmother picked up the strip of medication and threw it in the waste bin. She went to Shaykha's house and brought back a fresh egg laid by one of Shaykha's hens just that morning. She asked my father to write the letter ص on it nine times, in three rows of three each. And on a fourth line, beneath them, he was to write a word that didn't appear to mean anything, عجميطة. Next, my grandmother wrapped the egg in a linen rag and grilled it over the fire. She made me eat it. She put the eggshell back in the linen and bound it to my left arm. The next day, Sumayya pretended she was ill so that Gran would make the strange and wonderful hen egg for her. Sumayya pinched her cheeks until they were good and red, and stood next to the cooking stove until her skin felt like it was burning. Then she ran to my grandmother asking for *the egg*. But all my grandmother did was to pound some dried coriander together with some white sugar and feed it to her. Then she hung a fever talisman around Sumayya's neck, one that our grandmother Athurayyaa had written out for our father when he was a child. As soon as my grandmother was too busy feeding Sufyan to pay any attention to us, Sumayya opened up the talisman and we began reading it.

IN THE NAME OF GOD THE MERCIFUL AND BENEFICENT. GOD ALONE IS SUFFICIENT FOR US, AND GOD IS THE MOST PERFECT MANAGER OF OUR AFFAIRS. ALL POWER AND MIGHT IS UNTO GOD, GLORIED AND GREAT IS HE. WE SEND DOWN FROM THE QUR'AN THAT IN WHICH THERE IS A HEALING. O FEVER, APPROACH NOT MANSOUR IBN SALMAN.

Sumayya was furious because it wasn't her name that was written in the charm. She immediately shook off all signs of her fraudulent fever and went back to work building tiny grave sites for birds and lizards outside our house.

My story delighted Kuhl, and even Imran clapped his hands. "Tell us more!" But there wasn't anything more to tell. I hadn't gotten the fever again, but my mother's sobbing spells never stopped.

On the way back from Imran's flat, Kuhl put her hand in mine—a warm, soft hand that not long before had wiped away her beloved's sweat. We were silent; but it was a peaceful stillness that walked along between us. It was only a fever, after all, and he would recover quickly.

Two days later I went back there, on my own. I stood in front of the pub and looked up, trying to make out which window was Imran's. I stood there for a few moments, staring upward, trying to catch the winking reflections of light against the bead curtain. I went in and began climbing the stairs. Two floors up, suddenly, there were beads winking in my head, the string of beads belonging to the gypsy woman who used to go through our village begging for a few dried dates. I saw her blood running dark next to the necklace, which lay in pieces in the dirt, and I lost my balance. Kuhl's soft hand needed to be holding mine, to support me and keep me steady. I turned and walked down the stairs. As soon as I was in the street, I ran as fast as I could.

To Be Delirious with Joy

I was nine or ten, most likely, when I heard the name Kaaffa for the first time. I was in the courtyard, jumping rope. I didn't miss a single jump, I didn't stumble, even though my eyes were on Sumayya. She had stuffed her dress into her sirwal and climbed up the wall. She was swaying on the edge, gathering momentum to jump. Sumayya always competed with the neighborhood boys to see who could climb the fastest and jump the farthest from one wall to another. I tried once or twice to imitate her but the only results were cuts on my face and hands and knees. By now, I was satisfied with watching her and egging her on in those climbing races.

Sometimes Sumayya charged me with guarding the graveyard, which sat on a neglected bit of land a few meters from our house. As the sun beat down, I would have to stand there, and then stand there some more, guarding the tiny domes that Sumayya had built out of mud. We were afraid that one of the boys might attack them by riding his bike over and pulverizing them with the wheels. Or one of them might dig into the little mounds and extract the bird corpses and the lizard bodies and the "Abu Zayd" beetles that Sumayya took such pains to collect, burying them in tiny straight rows. She always arranged her bodies according to the type of corpse they were. I never did find out whether Sumayya had killed these tiny creatures so she could perform her rites on them, or whether she found them when they were already dead.

My grandmother had given up on scolding Sumayya. As usual these days, she was sitting quietly in the shade of the bitter orange tree, holding little Sufyan. He wasn't yet two. She fed him rice soaked in milk. Facing her sat Shaykha. Those were the days just before Shaykha lost her mind. My grandmother was trying to make Sufyan finish the bowl of milky rice, and he was trying to wriggle out of her grip. Shaykha was muttering, irritated, "Leave him, Bint Aamir. You're nearly seventy. You don't have the strength anymore to teach the little ones to mind you." My grandmother didn't react, leaving Shaykha to go on with her usual narrative. "We teach them to mind, we wear ourselves out for them, and then they go away. Look at my boy. I raised him, I lost sleep taking care of him, and where is he now? I don't know if he is alive or dead, but—may evil keep away from us—surely he's alive. He'll come back to me. Bewitched, ya habbat ayni. That infidel jinni woman snatched him out of my arms, apple of my eye! Ya habbat ayni! I never had any luck in my life,

Bint Aamir, no, I didn't. My family made me marry a man who was already sick. I lived with that man for six months and then he was gone, and he left me pregnant with that boy. Didn't leave me nothing else. No money, nothing, no one. La maal wa-la haal. He was a fine man, zayn, zayn! But he died. The fellow was snatched away from me, like he was a dream I only had once. That's what it was like, Bint Aamir, I tell you. He took me under his wing, and when I woke up he was gone. Like a dream at night, Bint Aamir, it's there and then it vanishes. Just there and gone, that's all I ever got from men."

Finally Bint Aamir snapped. "Well, at least he was there before he was gone, wasn't he!" she wailed into Shaykha's face.

Shaykha was silent. She made a show of trying to go after little Sufyan. The boy had perfected his skills, teasing the two women by tottering off and hiding, and rubbing his little food bowl in the dirt.

Sufyan was born at long last after my mother had had another two miscarriages. But, just when everyone around us thought for certain that now, finally, my mother would be delirious with joy, instead she went nearly mad with anguish. She never slept. It was the worst possible attack of postpartum depression, to the point that she could not even pick up the newborn, and she certainly could not nurse him. All night long she wandered from room to room in the darkness.

During the day, she cried, and between her sobs she was terror-stricken by the thought that she might be harming the baby. So my grandmother took him from his fright-stricken mother, moving his white bassinet into her room.

The neighbor women whispered among themselves that Bint Aamir was nursing the baby boy in secret as she had nursed his father, Mansour, before him. That her age—nearly seventy now—hadn't prevented the milk spouting from her nipples the moment she had a baby in her arms. But, just as my grandmother had raised my father, Mansour, in silence, now she raised my brother, Sufyan, in silence. She didn't offer a word of explanation to anyone.

By the time my grandmother and Shaykha were going after Sufyan with his bowl of milky rice, my mother had recovered from her depression and accepted the child. But things remained as before. My mother was absorbed in her own private occupations and my grandmother was immersed in the children. My grandmother never knew any happiness of her own. All her contentment was drawn from the happiness of the people for whom she cared.

Having managed to flee from my duties as guard over the bird-and-lizard graveyard and finally exhausted by my jump-rope exertions, I had collapsed onto the ground nearby. And so I heard what Shaykha said next. "If only your son, Mansour, loved his poor wife the way he loved that ingrate

Kaaffa then she would never have gone mad like this after having a baby. Praise be to God, that God showed His grace to her, and healed her."

Suddenly I was all ears. My whole body strained to hear. But Gran just muttered something, her voice stifled so that I could barely hear. "Don't start talking about Kaaffa," I think she said. "May God return your boy to you safe and sound."

A long sigh was Shaykha's only answer. She did not like it when my grandmother tried to bridle her. When my grandmother tried to prevent her from spreading news around, to keep things alive in people's memories as she liked to do.

I had to wait several more years before I learned anything of my father's love story, which was like nothing so much as a legend.

Young Love

Athurayyaa followed her husband. He was buried a stranger in Bombay, and she was buried shrouded in her daughter Hasina's cloth—the daughter who had emigrated a bride, and of whom there had been almost no news ever since. After his mother's death, the loneliness of the house closed in around Mansour. Bint Aamir's wailing for her friend put him in such a state of agony that he warned her she would lose her one good eye if she kept it up. He left the house, seeking companionship in the village alleyways.

Mansour was on that rocky, hard-to-climb path between adolescence and young adulthood. Somehow, he could not quite throw off the weight of his seventeen years and move on—as though he found the prospect of taking on his own personhood unbearable, not to mention the shop, the house, and the orchard he had inherited from his father. Caught miserably between sudden orphanhood and the hard glare of an abrupt freedom, he did not know how to be. He tried to keep his orphan self at bay, but he didn't know how to handle his freedom. He informed Bint Aamir that the shop would be closed for a period of mourning, and he roamed the streets and quarters of the village. He raced other boys his age through the little ponds left behind by rainstorms. He competed with them at hitting birds with a slingshot. He took out his father's rifle and polished it and began going on excursions into the desert for days at a time, returning only after he had bagged several birds or wild rabbits. Whenever he showed up, he found his mattress ready and his supper hot. Bint Aamir no longer pulled him by the ear, or even chastised him. That gave him a lump in his throat. He was a man now; and anyway, she was not his mother.

Summer came. Some Bedouin men visited Mansour to negotiate renting his date palms, whose yield they would sell. He agreed on one stand of date palms but retained the other. Now he began entertaining himself by going along with other youths his age to watch the Bedouin as they picked the dates, perched at the very tops of the palms. Their women clustered below, ready to pick up the fresh dates, filling their plaited palm-leaf baskets with the good ones and separating out the bad ones, which they would feed to their animals.

Watching them, it did not take him long to notice that among the women were some younger ones who, impatient with the ongoing work, exchanged glances and went off together to splash water over themselves at the falaj, in full view of him and his companions. And so he put on a show to end all shows. He lay down on the ground, spread his arms wide, and inhaled deeply, puffing out his bare chest, while his companions lined up across his body the live scorpions they had hunted for days. The lethal creatures crawled across his skin as if they were simply making a little day trip across their home territory.

The girls called out and acted terrified. Their families were not slow to scold them, and they had to hurry away. Except for one.

This girl went on watching the performance, motionless and silent. When Mansour had brushed off all the scorpions—none had harmed him in the slightest—she shrugged and walked off.

Mansour followed her, staring at her all the while. His long, steady gaze had been deepened and made more sensitive by this new orphan state, and then scarred by a rough passage into sudden manhood. But she did not return his tender, aching look. He followed her all summer long. All his other destinations ceased to be; she was the only one. Wherever she headed, that was what gave him direction: the fields by day, and her father's livestock enclosure out in the desert by night.

She was the robust color of early youth, she was the brimming freshness of dawn breaking, she was the delicate outline of a half-visible dream. Mansour's wishes were vast and his longing was fierce and hard to endure. Through him pulsed white-hot rivers of desire, and on them Kaaffa flooded his being, a storm wind that would not subside. She was a kaleidoscopic assemblage; she was bounty itself, joy, birds, little mirrors, cardamom, ginger, dates, ambergris, dawn prayers, the leopard skin hanging on the wall of his home that had been the gift of the twins.

He called out to her, as if he were just coming out of a stupendous, enormous dream. "Marry me!"

But she, Kaaffa, the picture of serenity, the cloudless sky, the summit of beauty . . . Kaaffa, beneath the lucent veil of her perfection, hid a wearied and restless nature, a bent for freedom as vast as the heavens. She had grown up in a sheltered open-air compound roofed with palm fronds not far from her father's animal enclosure. It was a happy place despite the presence of her father's wife and her father's wife's daughters, despite the smoky smell and the coal-blackened walls and the way the fragrance of bread buried in the sand always mingled with the camel-dung smell coming from nearby. There was one love in her life. Her father.

The summer ended. Coyly, she murmured words to Mansour, words that meant refusal and acceptance together. Words that promised abundance and absence. Words that said, "I am in my father's hands."

Pardoning

The father could not find any way to accept what his daughter, Kaaffa, had done. How could he forgive her for going away, going to the home of another man? True, that other man had done everything properly. He came with his relatives. They spoke long and proudly and well. They drank coffee together. He made his offer of a dowry. And they held a ceremony. But then—what she *did*. She went away. Or rather, she left him. *Him*. In his weakness, his need, his tenderness. She left him, this woman who was the closest woman to his heart, the most precious of any to his soul. She left him, and the only reason she left was to go to that other man, that stranger to them, who wanted her so much. Who wanted children by her, and who wanted it to be said, "That man has started a household now." And so she left him, her own father, a man who had no wants, no great ambitions, who loved her more than he loved his wife or all his sisters, daughters, she-camels, and livestock. She left him voluntarily, happily, finely dressed and adorned, for the other man. The stranger. The man from the village, the man of settled life, the hadari.

The man who, before the end of the very summer in which he had rented them the date palms with their yield, came and asked for their daughter. Came and drank coffee, and talked grandly, and paid the dowry that would buy gold bracelets and earrings and sumptuous silks.

In his pain, he groaned, "What is there in gold and silk? I could have sold a few goats and bought her more gold than this, and softer silks. But she didn't ask for anything. Instead, she took her dowry and she bought what she bought and she went off happily enough, willing to go to another man's household."

The father did not tell anyone of the pain in his heart. He did not show how bitterly betrayed he felt. He knew what people would say, if he did. He would hear the same words over and over. "Sunnat al-hayat. Marriage is God's plan for our lives. It's the way of the world. It's written for her. The seeds of her womb—that's her destiny." To hell with them all! Surely that plan was not meant to deprive him of the person dearest to his heart? And what was the point of growing seeds if someday they would leave her, as she had left him?

Long sleepless nights elapsed. He could not accept it; how could he forgive her? Even if *she* wouldn't be able to see that this stranger-man would not care if her feet poked out of the blanket—he wouldn't care enough to see that they were tucked in again. And how would the stranger-man know that she always got ill if her feet were allowed to get cold? When Mansour had been no more than a silly young boy, her father was already heating olive oil to rub into her feet every night until they were safely beyond the winter. If these two were to sleep out in the open, for instance while moving from one place to another, how would that town boy know that he must mark out the space around the mat on which she slept, digging a shallow little trench to keep the scorpions from attacking her? Would he examine the place closely enough, looking out for telltale holes in the ground and burrows in the sand before spreading out the mat on which *his* daughter would sleep? Would he brush protective charms across her forehead and would he know the right incantations? If the cold crept upward from the soles of her feet and she did get sick, what would the stranger-man do? What would he do? He repeated the question to himself and began to heave and sob. His wife figured it was his night ravings again. She shook him awake. He couldn't help himself, asking her about incantations and spells and getting ill from the cold. His wife was much younger than he was. He always found it hard to take, when she looked at him this way, pitying his old age. And so he would retreat from his odd, insistent questions. But this time she did not show any sympathy, nor even pity. "Do you really think your daughter's husband is an ignorant old Bedouin shaykh like you are?" she asked him grimly. "This is a civilized boy, from the town, and he knows all the things that you don't know. And he has a big house and a shop and orchards. So, for a start, he doesn't need to make the girl sleep out in the open."

He was silent. He was embarrassed. Very. About the olive oil and the amulets and the trenches in the sand. He kept his questions to himself and he kept himself from weeping. But he didn't know how he was going to ever forgive his daughter, who had chosen this stranger-man and gone away with him, gone away to his house.

Curiosity

Now that Kaaffa was with him, Mansour felt like he was standing under a waterfall, embracing its pure fullness, its energy. He felt cleansed; he felt perfumed and molded by the spray that rose as the water hit the ground. He felt like a well-watered tree. He felt replete, overflowing with everything.

She was standing outside the waterfall: that is what it felt like for Kaaffa. Her back was pressed against the rocks as she looked across and through the waterfall at him while remaining completely dry. There was nothing to drink in; she was simply looking. Or trying to look. The view, from outside the waterfall, was a gaze through water. It was a foggy vista. That is how she saw him. Foggy, beneath the luxuriant spray of the waterfall she made.

She met his worship of her with a face that seemed elsewhere, features that were absent. This husband—someone whose bed she had awoken one morning to find herself in, merely because there had been a festive evening with lots of singing and a great deal of food. This husband was a person one might feel a bit curious about, but that was all. Only a few months passed before Kaaffa lost even the speck of curiosity she previously had. She didn't feel any interest in discovering anything further. And now she did not know what to do in this big house, with this slightly overgrown adolescent who insisted on washing her feet and rubbing them with rose petals, or with this mother of his who had not even given birth to him. A mother who watched his madness in silence and seemed to have taken on the management of the orchards he had inherited and sat in the shop in his stead.

His love had been an idea, a thought, a fancy. Yes, it had an urgency to it; yes, it was an insistent, tormenting idea. But it was a semblance more than anything based in the here and now. Often, just being with him made her restless and uneasy. She felt as though she were walking hopelessly and aimlessly through a tract of land that stretched on in every direction, where every clump of vegetation had exactly the same shape as the next one and all of them were exactly the same shade of green.

Now and then, the tone of his voice sent rays of warm joy shooting into her chest, but the words themselves made her uncomfortable, throwing a dark pall over those bright rays and choking them out.

She was tired of being worshipped. She wanted something a little more human. Something more fun, but also more serious than this repetitive game of abject adoration. She wanted to be surprised, but it seemed that everything had been sketched out in advance. She wanted to be dazzled, to feel the anticipation of the wait. But he never made her wait. Every moment, every new thing—it was always ready, always polished and shiny and sitting at her feet.

She was longing for the desert, for a run through the sand, chasing after lizards, tending flocks of sheep and grooming the she-camels. She missed singing with her father as they sat on the tussocks nearby on moonlit evenings. She was bored with the silk that this husband wanted her to put on every night, and she was tired of living in a house surrounded by walls that looked endlessly high to her. The price of deification was being paid by her body and her spirit, both held lifeless in these walls. On the one hand, her body was sacred; on the other, it was the object of desire. Trying to fulfill both demands at once was exhausting her. She found it painful, too.

The Scorpion

After Kaaffa left, Mansour fell to pieces.

He buried himself in the soil of the courtyard trying to put out the searing pain in his body, but he could not extinguish it. She left behind a single tarha, only because she forgot it. He spread that wrap out and slept on it. He buried his nose in it, and he rubbed his body with it until its color was all but gone. He dipped it into the falaj and squeezed the water into his mouth. But none of this gave him any relief.

On cold nights he paced back and forth along the rise from where he could see the fire in her father's shelter. He threw sand over himself as he called out her name in a voice now hoarse with weeping. But she did not come at the sound of her name welling up from his raw throat.

His hair grew long. Bint Aamir began washing it regularly, getting the dirt out and braiding it as if he were a little boy again. Grimly, she spread out Kaaffa's tarha in the sun until it was dry yet again. And then Mansour would wet it again and squeeze the water into his mouth. She fed him chilled camel's milk and an infusion made from the leaves of the chaste tree. She boiled passionflower in water to calm the fire in his gut.

People came to visit him and he shut the door in their faces. Rayyaa and Raayah stood at the door and called out, "Here is the punishment for a man who celebrates his wedding when his folks haven't even been in their graves for a full twelve months." Bint Aamir opened the door and threw the dust-filled leopard skin at them. "What's the punishment for those who forget the charity they're given?" she barked.

Mansour, already half-mad, continued to deteriorate. Until one morning he woke up in terrible pain. A scorpion had stung him.

No one could believe that Mansour had suffered a scorpion sting. But the pain of it got him back on his feet. He recovered. He hid Kaaffa's tarha, by now in tatters, in his wardrobe, and he reopened his father's shop.

Imran

The Ukrainian waitress at the Three Monkeys Café was gone. A woman from Poland had taken her place.

I told Imran that my grandmother had a green thumb, and he laughed—that slightly painful laugh of his. He himself, he said, who had grown up a peasant, did not have a green thumb. His father always had to replant the seedlings his son put in the ground.

What was in his mind when he said that? What was in Kuhl's mind as she lifted her head from her notebook upon hearing him say these things? Probably she was remembering the pastures and fields she had seen in animations when she was little, of Heidi and Sandybell. Probably Imran was remembering his father's slaps and kicks. Kuhl could not see the traces the whip and the iron spike had left on his spirit; she had only followed the marks left on his body, tracing them with her lips and then considering them healed. They had already known each other for many months when Imran first told her about his father. She was the one who brought up the subject. She saw the scars on his body, and so she asked.

Before she ever saw his body, she had tossed with him on the bed of her imagination, the flames of longing illuminating his form in her mind like a vivid divination. When she saw the reality, she put her arms around him and cried. She cried until her tears had drowned all the Punjabi kurtas whose tailoring she had had no part in selecting, and the somber Mary Jane flats that were the only shoes her mother thought appropriate for girls who were so plain. All these things that she had taken for granted, had thought were deeply ingrained parts of her—this tsunami of tears swept them away, altering her landscape once and forever.

And me? What was in my head? My grandmother's image.

In his crushing solitude and pain, after the scorpion stung him, Mansour was suddenly conscious of the quiet, steady tenderness of his mother Bint Aamir, as he never had been before. It was almost a shock to truly recognize that she had only one working eye. The idea of eyeglasses suddenly came to him. He bought a pair, with whorly, knotted red frames. They were small for her head size, pressing in on both sides when she put them on. But they were eyeglasses. And they were Mansour's gift, and she had never loved anything or anyone in her life as much as she loved Mansour. He had brought them to her without being asked, and she wore them without voicing any complaint. Whatever traces of resentful envy she had against Rayyaa and Raayah—the humpbacked and the nearsighted—melted from her heart.

After his divorce from Kaaffa, Mansour remained alone and broken, despite his return to the shop. My grandmother tried to persuade him to expand the orchard. She wanted him to reclaim more land, and she would teach him the secrets of growing things: that perfect dark shade of green to look for, how much to water. She would show him how living plants longed for company and interaction. It wasn't the usual that she had in mind—ordinary groves like those he had inherited from his father, all date palms with hardly even one lemon or mango tree among them. She dreamed of row after row of medicinal plants, aloe and rank-smelling mkhisa alongside basil and jasmine, orchids, wild lavender, and small ornamental trees. Tens and tens of fruit trees, she thought, surrounded by patches of onions, potatoes, tomatoes, and sweet peppers. In her dreams she heard the gurgling of the canal as it sent water into the sinews of every single plant, renewing the living vigor there.

But Mansour chose trade instead. He strengthened his ties to the merchants in Sur. He learned the secrets, the techniques, the art of it all. He was well-positioned to benefit from the opening of the economy. His trade flourished and after only a few years he engaged himself to the daughter of one of Sur's big merchants. My mother.

Her father set a condition: his daughter was not to be removed from the city of Sur. That suited my father's inclinations—or his dreams—at the time. He'd grown bored and weary of the torpor of his hometown, and he had got it into his head that he wanted to build a house on the coast. Bint Aamir refused to move out of the old house. "I'm not leaving the House of Salman," she declared. When Mansour's bride came to her, she kissed Bint Aamir's brow and said, "Come with us, Maah. Mansour can't live without you." So it was that our grandmother left her hometown for the second time in her life, having left the first time as a young woman heading toward Muscat in a goods truck to meet Dr. Thoms.

The fields she dreamed of were never planted. Mansour sold the orchards he had inherited and devoted himself to commerce. My grandmother emptied her dreams into the garden at the Sur home, where the soil lacked richness.

"The worst that can happen to a peasant is no longer owning the land," observed Imran.

Neither Imran nor his father ever truly owned the land they farmed. It had been mortgaged and the debt was never cleared. When Imran got the Aga Khan scholarship to study medicine, his father began to dream that Imran would come back a doctor and would pay off the money that was owed. But his father died while Imran was overseas.

Tall, lean, and hard, humiliated constantly by his father,

as he received the news of his success at getting the scholarship, spattered with the soil of the land they did not own, Imran vowed silently that he would never return to this village where he had grown up. Even in those nights when the snow and ice were at their worst, and he longed for home the most—those nights when his mother's tears kept him from sleeping, as he remembered her trying to treat the wounds left by the father's whip and his hot iron skewer on the body of the youth he had been then—Imran swore he would never go back. But destiny had made a different vow.

The Heart Is Made of Clay and Water

Mansour's heart might as well have been a clay jug filled with water, which Kaaffa broke simply with her indifferent gaze. The water drained out and it would never come back. The earthenware jug could never be filled again. When, deep in the night, she began waking up in terror, crying that she had had nightmares meant to warn her, they could only have one interpretation: she must not stay with Mansour, he was beside himself. He would rip his sleeve off rather than remove it from under her head, to keep her from waking, curled around herself on the very edge of the bed.

When she arrived at her father's shelter, now a divorced woman at her own insistence, her father slaughtered livestock and held a feast to celebrate the return of his beloved daughter. Once again, facing his young wife, he could right the balance. He and his daughter, Kaaffa—long ago orphaned by her mother, and who had now left her husband to return to her father's embrace—sat again on one tray of the balance. His wife—so much in love with her own youth—and her daughters sat on the other tray. His equilibrium had returned. He began to sleep well again.

Mansour's earthenware heart was put back together, but the water of life was gone forever. More than a decade later, when he married the daughter of the Sur merchant, he was an affectionate and respectful husband. Sometimes he even spoiled her a bit. But there was no life to it, no freshness, not a whiff of the passion that had pushed him to tear his own sleeves and to rub Kaaffa's feet with whole bushes of rose petals.

No one knew what happened to Kaaffa after her father died. Sometime before, he had stopped racing with her on camelback. His voice still sounded out hoarsely as they sang together on those moon-filled nights. Now his hands shook when he patted her on the head. She rubbed his hands with warmed olive oil and sang little lullabies to him. And then he aged to the point where he could no longer tell the past from the present. He started calling her by her mother's name. When he was paralyzed, no longer able to move at all, his wife had to keep him in diapers. It was a terrible blow to his self-esteem, which he had always worked so hard to maintain in her presence. He couldn't find any means of preserving his pride, now demolished by old age and infirmity, other than by divorcing her. So he abruptly pronounced the formula for divorce. Without any fuss, she left his room and moved to the other end of the house with her daughters. Now Kaaffa was responsible for managing his old age, and his dignity, for the remaining days of his life.

When he died, Kaaffa left the compound. No one knew where she went.

The Holy Night of Revelation

We finished the apple tart and ice cream. Feeling relaxed, I stretched my legs out a little. Imran noticed my red shoes, and said their color intrigued him. They were made of leather, I told him. Natural skin. Then there was silence. Kuhl went back to her notebook and I exchanged a few words with the Polish waitress. She told me she was studying biology and had worked as a window cleaner and child minder to pay her university fees. Her dream was to stay on in Western Europe, she said.

Imran spoke up suddenly. "Those shoes! As if they are made from the skins of oppressed peoples."

I stared at his glossy brown shoes. I didn't say anything. I was remembering his plastic wardrobe opposite the bead curtain. I imagined the shirts slapping against each other inside, like flags caught in a strong gust of wind, but one whose effects were nevertheless invisible, as though it were a whirlwind welling up only inside me. Hearing the sound of the shirts flapping in the wind sent me to the sea, to the slap of sails on never-ending voyages, to a lost ship raising the flag in *Love in the Time of Cholera* to the swirling and eddying of the ocean, sea shanties, the whale in the story of Sinbad the Sailor, the glint of strange and far-off stars. I tugged at my spirit, which was stumbling over the buttons of Imran's shirts in his wardrobe, getting tangled up in Kuhl's spirit on the way and stumbling over it as well.

Kuhl was bursting with tenderness, but it looked to me like Imran was trying to fend off her affection in self-defense. He always tries to keep a distance between himself and others, I thought. Not because he believed he was better than they were, but because he was wary of them. Wherever he landed, he seemed to create around himself an aura of opacity and silence, keeping everyone a fierce arm's length away. Kuhl broke open the aura, and forced this unyielding arm—which still showed the traces of the glowing iron spike, the father's hateful anger—to encircle her. But her route to this arm scarred by the seal of cruelty was a tough and rocky one. Even now, with the first anniversary of their secret marriage approaching, waves of doubt about whether this devotion was real and lasting, since he had never known the like—or alternatively, known fears about its very strength—would crest and break over him, sweeping him somewhere far away.

Imran was not inattentive to others. In fact, he paid more attention, and cared more, than people thought. They believed that his apparent indifference to others meant he cared only about his studies. In fact, his was a profound curiosity about people. But it was a curiosity he kept concealed, or at least camouflaged. It was a curiosity that extended to me.

He was clever—he could even be sly—but he was not out to deceive anyone. Kuhl recognized his pure intentions, as I did, too. It was just that he was so tightly swathed in the winding cloths of a terrible, frightening childhood. The cringing affection of an abased mother had not been able to protect him from all of that humiliation. Her powerlessness had only intensified it.

In his village, everything was made from dried mud. Houses, livestock enclosures, the walls around every field, the primary school. Even the emaciated animals were covered with splatters of dried mud. The one structure built of stone was the imam's shrine. From its hidden inner chamber the expected Mahdi was to emerge. This savior would flood the world with justice, for it had become a world of tyranny. No one knew exactly where in the shrine the vault sat. Imran started going there every night. He lifted the worn-out carpets and inspected the stone floor. He put his ear to every inch of the place, knocking and tapping the walls, but the shrine never revealed the secret of its vault.

On Laylat al-Qadr, he saw a light coming through the cracks in the floor, and he heard the sound of weeping. He put out his hands in the darkness—the hands of a young man, burned and scarred by the father's iron spikes. He tried to jiggle the stones, and then to push them. They slid open, and there was the vault. Imran squeezed himself into it easily and dropped lightly, like a bird landing gently on the ground. The vault was paved in silver. He saw the seated imam, poised on one pan of an enormous scale, balanced by an equivalent weight in gold. He was wearing a white robe embroidered with gold threads and a tall cap studded with carnelian. Imran stood before him, and the imam put out his hand, diamond and ruby rings on his fingers. The hand touched the burn marks left by the hot iron skewer, and the wounds left by the leather whip scourging Imran's body. The imam ordered his followers to catch the young man's tears in a worked silver bowl. When the imam dipped his hand in the bowl, the tears turned into pearls, which his acolytes then dropped into Imran's pockets. They lit his way out with torches. The door to the vault closed. It did not open again.

The Fiancé

After my grandmother buried her friend—our elderly neighbor Shaykha—she took to spending the late afternoons on the stone bench in front of our house, staring at her neighbor's front entrance, the metal door shut and locked. The key was with Gran. After all, Shaykha's son, who had emigrated so long ago, might be set free by the jinni women of the West, and come back one day to open up his mother's house—the mother who went raving mad and died waiting for him.

One overcast day, as the afternoon was darkening, an old man appeared. He was a stooped, fragile figure, and his beard had gone white. When he saw her sitting there, he rapped on the door with his cane and called out, "Gharib wa-atshaan! I'm a stranger here, and I'm thirsty!" My grandmother waved at him to sit down. She brought him a glass of water, a plate of dates, and a little pot of coffee. He settled himself comfortably on the bench in front of old Shaykha's house. He ate and drank. He began telling my grandmother how he had lost his way returning from the hospital. The driver he had hired set him down in this village instead of his own. He didn't notice at first, and wondered why he could not find his way home. And then he realized that he was in a different village.

My grandmother told him about her neighbor who had died; about Shaykha's longing that her son would come back; about the trees she had planted that had given fruit, about the wonders of the bitter orange tree that didn't bear fruit until my grandmother patted and rubbed it with her own hands; about her son, Mansour, and his wife from Sur, the big city, and his children; about their first home when they were married, on the coast at Sur, and then how they had moved back to the village when the woman couldn't bear the smell of the sea during her second pregnancy, which didn't end in miscarriage. About little Sufyan's aversion to formula and his wild love for chocolate even before his teeth were fully grown in; about her son Mansour's trips to the Emirates with his children, and the little gifts he brought back—from bottles of perfume and hair creams to the combs that the girls always gave her. About the lengths of fabric and the wraps his wife brought her, and how she knew perfectly well that Mansour bought all these things and then handed them out to his wife and children to give to her. About the one time she traveled with them to the Emirates. She didn't like it there at all, and decided to stay home after that, even when they headed off in the summers. Then she told him the latest news in the village.

When the man got to his feet, it was evening. She had persuaded one of the neighbors to drive him to his own village. As he was stooping to climb into the car, he asked her what was her name, and who were her family? When she told him, the man began to laugh. His mouth was open so wide that she could see his toothless gums. Before she could get too annoyed at the sight, or at the sound of his cackle, he said, "You? You're Bint Aamir? The horseman's girl? I tried to marry you fifty years ago, but your papa refused me."

He kept on laughing, even as the car started up and took off. My grandmother stood there, staring after it.

That was the night my grandmother turned elderly. Through her few remaining years, the body that had been so strong and erect would slowly deteriorate, collapsing into lameness and violating the norms of suitable conduct that she had preserved, in all dignity, throughout her life.

Triangle

Imran traveled to his village—a village without a name, somewhere in the Pakistani hinterland. Kuhl lost her equilibrium.

She wanted to write to him—the *little love notes* that you hear about in songs. She wanted him to know that in his isolation and distress over a life of deprivation and want, that her spirit was hovering, enfolding him. That if she could not change a single line in what was written for him, her fingers were long enough that even from here she could touch his hair and stroke it.

She wanted to talk to him about desire. How it burns, truly burns, how the stinging pain of it surprises you, reaching the deepest recess of your heart, and you don't understand how to transcend it.

Kuhl talks to me about this desire that burns, and I imagine you. I imagine you through her eyes, Imran. I imagine your hair, at the line where it meets your neck, and I imagine myself stroking it. And I dream that you are feeling—in this precise moment—my finger twisting a short lock of your hair around itself. That your fingers are spreading my hair out across a white mattress, to look at it. I imagine my hair twirling like the spinning swings in amusement parks. I am mad for you; I am mad with you. I am Kuhl, and I want to give you the milk from my breasts, so that you will be my son. To give you the honey of my womanhood, so that you will be my man. To feel you patting me on the shoulder, and then you will become my father.

Imran traveled, his body all gentle feeling and all hardness, displaying the utmost unconcern toward humanity and concealing the most vivid interest in people. He traveled when death had just closed his father's eyes—those eyes that had always and ever radiated a fiery accusation at his son. Imran was always in the wrong. Accused of error if he acted; at fault if he intended to act; sinning if he did not act at all. His very presence was subject to danger. When his father died and the danger vanished, Imran finished his degree and traveled immediately to his village, where he would become the man of the household.

Kuhl was waiting.

The two of them led lives in which imagination occupied a very narrow margin. They loved each other, they were partners in desire, and so they married. But I, standing at the head of the triangle, had let imagination fill the whole space of my life. I *made* the imaginary my life. I loved them both, and I desired their union, and our union. I was happy enough living with imagination. It was imagination that developed and tended my strength of will, while reality was smashing it to bits.

Kuhl and I are alone in the Three Monkeys Café. I want to speak. But silence is what we have. I want to ask about the corner of his mouth. About his fear of people. About how he left without making any promises. I want Kuhl, this sad woman across from me, to shout out his name. And I want to shout with her. Imran! I want to say something about different cloth, about how the weave of his trousers was not spun along with the weave of her skirt, and so it all unraveled. If only it hadn't come apart. If only grace had come down from a merciful heaven allowing me to cleanse their two hearts every dawn. Every dawn.

But what we had was silence. It is not merciful, silence, nor is talk.

In the beginning, my spirit roved across her face. In the end, my spirit wandered restlessly amid the walls of the Three Monkeys Café.

And then my spirit landed on your balcony. It dived into your pillow, drank from your cup, buried itself amid your books. It embraced your wife. The abandoned body, Imran. Kuhl's body. A body whose steps are no longer steady. Its gaze is not steady. And the roaming spirit cannot come back, nor can it rest.

The source of my companionship—what I mean to say is, *my solitude*. Don't touch my spirit as it moves restlessly through your café, for it is nothing but a sad shadow now. My friend—what I want to say is, *my beloved*. My beloved— what I need to say is, *my partner, my other half. My husband.*

Sheets

When my grandmother told me the tale of the lion who gently offered his back to carry the load of firewood for the man with the mean wife, she said, "If the Lord brings a catastrophe down on His servant, the Lord compensates His servant for it with something else." When I got older and she was no longer braiding my hair, no longer strong enough to walk, and no longer able to make out anything but vague shapes with her one good eye, she told me and Sumayya another story. This one was about her father, in the year that Sa'id bin Taymur became ruler of Muscat. Clan Hammuda of Jaalaan sent word secretly to her father. They hoped to tempt him to join them in seceding and proclaiming independence. They craved his heroic persona and his singular courage. He craved the money funneled to them by the House of Saud. His brothers were furious, because Clan Hammuda followed a different religious line. He didn't pay them any attention. Sharifa, his mother—who was known as Sharifa al-Aziza, Sharifa the Noble, because her family had famously accrued such sharaf and 'izz, honor and glory—cut off all communication with him. He shrugged that off, and entered a losing battle against the sultan and the British. He came back suffering from a shrapnel wound in the shoulder and the death of white Dahim, his favorite mare. He lost everything he had, because he had pawned it all off to buy weapons. The shame of it kept him away from the men's gatherings. He sat at home, kicking at the walls in frustration and punching anyone who came near. On the day he realized that he must sell the last of his horses to feed his children, his wife observed sharply that his son was now old enough to support himself and his one-eyed sister.

I didn't really listen to the story. At the time, my exams were looming and I had my eyes on a scholarship to study in Europe. Sumayya wasn't interested either. The handsome young man who had just gotten his degree in Australia had presented himself, and she was longing for the promised bliss. We left my grandmother's room quietly. She didn't say, "Don't go." My mother asked us, "Does Maah need a bath?" We nodded. She called the servant.

That was the last story I heard my grandmother tell.

I was dreaming, and flocks of swooping birds woke me up. What I felt against my cheek was the rough weave of my grandmother's garments. Not for the first time, I recollected that I had not really said goodbye to her before I traveled. I got out of bed to go over to the telephone. How could I have forgotten to say goodbye? Halfway between my bed and the telephone I remembered, suddenly, that she had died. And I remembered the sheets.

The sheets were collected quickly. Green, brown, cream, striped, worked, plain, new, old; some with tassels on their edges and others with hastily done lines of stitching along the hems. They were all lifted, held together or singly, by this crowd of women who formed a square of fluttering sheets around the bier. The women knotted the corners, and their hands, keeping the sheet-curtains high, came together at the knots to form a tent with no gaps. But something was not quite as tightly joined as it should have been. What was taking place under the protective veil of this square, improvised tent formed by sheets was not curtained at all. The heavy, musty-smelling cloth with the tassels along the edge was meant to open only enough so that one of the women assigned to wash the corpse could fetch another bucket of water, or the perfumer could stick her head just far enough out to ask where the aloe was, or to request a bit more camphor. But instead, it opened to every little puff of wind—and to curious glances, now and then, from the women who were holding up the improvised square tent. Some of them were relaxing their grip, lowering their arms, stealing little glances at the unclothed body of the dead woman. Since the deceased was not a young person whose face had been smashed up in a car accident, nor an invalid whose body carried the raw scars of a recent operation, there was not much to look at that could furnish later conversations, in whispered moments when the women were sitting together, or during louder moments at family gatherings not yet muted by the presence of a body in a shroud.

The corpse washers and the perfumers announced that their work was done. The women who had been holding the sheets aloft now rested their arms. As tired as they might be, none of them seemed too fatigued to display the strain to their backs or rub their hands together vigorously, ridding themselves of the numbness. Someone gathered up the pile of sheets and took them all away.

And so Bint Aamir came into that time in which there is no air, no light, no end. The time against which every life appears unbelievably short, and swiftly gone, even the life of my grandmother.

The Valiant Horseman

She was a child who wore twenty braids oiled lovingly with myrtle. Her cheeks were daubed with saffron and her eyes were little stars. She had a house, and that house sat amid small fields. Behind it was a stable for the horses. She had a father who was a renowned man of the horse, and a mother who was all gentleness, and a loving brother, and a name.

The mother had not yet died, the father had not yet married another woman, and there were not yet so many hungry mouths clustered around him. The father had not yet lost all of his stallions, and the cost of a sack of rice had not shot up to a hundred qirsh. She had not yet lost her eye, and would not have heard her father mutter, "I will never marry off this girl and hear her husband's family calling her the One-Eyed."

She was a playful child, her twenty braids flying behind her as her father took her riding behind him on his favorite horse, sparkling white Dahim. Her brother fixed a covered saddle on his gray donkey and pushed them both up the little hill ahead of him. She laughed until tears wet her cheeks and the saffron ran down her face, painting stripes on her neck.

She would call together the little girls in the neighborhood and give them their orders. One girl was to scrape and smooth and polish the little sticks of wood with a knife. Another would forage scraps of cloth from their mothers' sewing baskets. A third would gather the eggs deposited by the tiny fish in the falaj. Yet another would look for stray strands of wool. When they had all brought their precious finds, setting everything on the ground for her inspection, the little factory could go into action. It was not over until a row of wooden dolls displayed their bewilderingly colorful frocks, earrings made of fish roe, woolen hair, and finally the eyes that were kohl-penciled in.

She and her friends sang to the dolls and the dolls sang back to them. They danced, and the dolls danced around them. They stuffed the bottom halves of their dishdashas into their sirwals and clambered onto the fallen date-palm trunks, which immediately turned into the backs of horses beneath their warm bodies, taking off into the air. She was the fastest, and behind her the girls all sang. Buniyya ya buniyya . . .

Little lass, O little lass, her father's the hero
gallant
Master of his tall white steed, in goodness
never errant

She came home spent and covered in dust. Her mother bathed her in the falaj and draped a necklace of jasmine flowers around her neck. When her father came in, she took a deep breath of happiness. He would pat her on the head, and she would tell him, "You smell bad." Though he rarely smiled, his smile for her was genuine as he said, "Perfume is for women. Men have the sweat of horses, and the smell of gunpowder."

His hair was long and seldom washed. His beard was sparse. She dreamed he would let her touch his hair. She could make it like she made the wool into the hair on her dolls' heads. But she was too much in awe of him. And the furthest he ever went to show his approval was when he patted her on the head and gave her that special rare smile.

The women had all composed poems praising his courage and his grace. She had memorized a few of them, secretly, to escape the mother's jealousy. Flying into the air on the date-palm trunk turned stallion, sailing on the palm-fiber-rope swing out into the field, she always repeated the words to herself.

To see his figure as dusk fell
  So tall and strong, the valiant one!
May God protect and guard him well:
  Noblest Aamir, Sh'rifa's son

© Ilham Alharthi

JOKHA ALHARTHI was the first Omani woman to have a novel translated into English. *Celestial Bodies* went on to win the Man Booker International Prize and became an international bestseller. Alharthi is the author of three collections of short fiction, three children's books, and four novels in Arabic. She completed a PhD in classical Arabic poetry in Edinburgh and teaches at Sultan Qaboos University in Muscat.

© Bette Chapman

MARILYN BOOTH holds the Khalid bin Abdullah Al Saud Chair for the Study of the Contemporary Arab World at Oxford University. In addition to her academic publications, she has translated many works of fiction from the Arabic, most recently *The Penguin's Song* and *No Road to Paradise*, both by Lebanese novelist Hassan Daoud, and *Voices of the Lost* by Hoda Barakat. Her translation of *Celestial Bodies* won the Man Booker International Prize.